Ladies of St. Cecelia Guild

Marshall Ladies' Choicest and Best

Ladies of St. Cecelia Guild

Marshall Ladies' Choicest and Best

ISBN/EAN: 9783337380694

Printed in Europe, USA, Canada, Australia, Japan

Cover: Foto ©Andreas Hilbeck / pixelio.de

More available books at **www.hansebooks.com**

4

WEIGHTS AND MEASURES.

Two and a half teaspoonfuls make one tablespoonful.

Four tablespoonfuls make one wineglassful.

Two wineglassfuls make one gill.

Two gills make one teacupful.

Two teacupfuls make one pint.

Four teaspoonfuls salt make one ounce.

One and a half teaspoonfuls granulated sugar make one ounce.

Two tablespoonfuls flour make one ounce.

Two cups, or one pint, granulated sugar weighs about one pound.

One scant quart wheat flour weighs about one pound.

Ten ordinary sized eggs weigh about one pound.

A piece of butter the size of an egg weighs about one and a half ounces.

Two cups of butter weigh about one pound.

SOUPS.

CREAM OF POTATO SOUP.

One quart milk heated in double boiler. Put in an onion and few pieces of celery. Skim out when milk is thoroughly hot. Have ready one cup finely mashed potato. Stir it into the potato; also, lump of butter, and salt to taste. Serve very hot.

POTATO SOUP.

Six large potatoes, boiled and put through a colander; add one cup cream, three pints hot milk, one-half cup butter. Beat one egg light; add one tablespoon flour and a little cold milk to thin it; add celery, parsley, and onion, if liked. Strain through sieve, and serve hot.

MRS. O. E. JENKINS, Chicago.

CREAM POTATO SOUP.

One quart milk, six large potatoes, one stalk celery, one onion, one tablespoon butter. Put milk, celery and onion on to boil. Boil potatoes thirty minutes; pour water off and mash fine; salt to taste; add to milk. Whip a cup of cream and add just before serving.

MRS. JOHN L. WATSON.

CORN SOUP.

Six ears of corn, scraped; one-half cup cream; one tablespoon butter; one pint milk; one-half cup water. Boil corn in water twenty minutes, being careful not to let burn. Add butter, cream and milk. Let come to a boil. Season to taste.

MRS. V. B. SEWARD.

VEGETABLE SOUP.

Scrape two carrots. an onion, one-fourth head cabbage, and two turnips.   Cut them in small pieces. Put them in a large saucepan, with a little butter and water.   Let it cook one-half hour, then cut three good sized potatoes fine, and add.   Take meat out of soup kettle, skim off grease, put vegetables into it, and let cook another half hour.   In the language of the average school girl, "It's perfectly lovely!"

NOODLES FOR SOUP.

Break two eggs into bowl; beat until light; add pinch salt; then add flour until you have very stiff dough.   Turn on molding board, and work until as smooth as glass.   Roll very thin, and cut in very narrow strips.   Having prepared some good veal, chicken, or other broth, well seasoned, one-half hour before dinner drop in noodles.   Be sure soup is boiling.   If noodles are made according to directions they will be found superior to macaroni.

CHICKEN CREAM SOUP.

One chicken, season with salt and pepper; one onion (if you like); four quarts water boiled down to two quarts; two egg yolks (boiled hard), chopped fine; one pint sweet milk; one pint cream.   When chicken is done, take breast and chop fine.   Put chopped meat and egg in broth, and simmer a few minutes; then add milk boiling hot.

MRS. A. D. EMERY, Minneapolis.

TOMATO SOUP.

One quart of tomatoes; one of water. Stew until soft. Add small teaspoon soda; allow to effervesce, and add one quart boiling milk; salt, butter and pepper to taste.

MRS. W. B. THORBURN.

VERMICELLI SOUP.

One quart chicken stock, one quart beef stock, one-third pound vermicelli cooked in clear water twenty minutes; butter, salt and pepper to taste.

MRS. S. N. HARRINGTON.

NORWEGIAN SOUP.

One large cup sago, one pound raisins, one pound currants, one pound best prunes, one tablespoon vinegar, pinch salt and several cinnamon sticks. Water to make like thick sauce; cook several hours; sugar to taste. Thin at the last with one pint good red wine; take out cinnamon sticks; keep thinned with water.

MRS. L. M. LANGE.

TOMATO BISQUE.

One quart of stewed tomatoes, either fresh or canned, one quart of water and one medium-sized onion sliced very fine. Heat thoroughly, and put through a sieve or fine strainer, so as to make perfectly smooth; stir in a half teaspoon of soda, add one-half bottle of Heinz catsup, two teaspoons of sugar; season with salt, pepper and two tablespoons of butter. Heat to boiling point, and thicken with two tablespoons of flour. Serve in cups with crackers buttered and browned in the oven.

MRS. H. J. MOWREY, Watertown, S. D.

FISH AND OYSTERS.

STEWED OYSTERS (IN MILK OR CREAM).

Drain the liquor from two quarts of oysters; mix with it a small teacupful of hot water; add a little salt and pepper, and set it over the fire in a sauce pan. Let it boil up once; put in the oysters; let them come to a boil, and when they "ruffle" add two tablespoonfuls of butter. The instant it is melted and well stirred in, put in a pint of boiling milk, and take the sauce pan from the fire. Serve while hot, with oyster or cream crackers. If thickening is preferred, stir in a little flour, or two tablespoonfuls of crackers.

FISH TURBOT.

Boil a white-fish until tender; remove bones and sprinkle with pepper and salt. Heat one pint of milk and thicken with three tablespoons of flour. When cool, add two eggs, three tablespoons of butter and a bit of chopped onion or parsley. Place a layer of fish in a baking dish, then a layer of sauce, until full. Cover the top with bread crumbs and bake half an hour.   MRS. JOHN L. WATSON.

DRY OYSTER STEW.

Take six to twelve large oysters and cook them in half a pint of their own liquor; season with butter and white pepper; cook for five minutes, stirring constantly. Serve in hot soup plates or bowls.

SCALLOPED OYSTERS.

Have ready about a pint bowl of cracker crumbs. Butter a deep earthen dish; put a layer of cracker crumbs on the bottom; wet this with some of the oyster liquor; next have a layer of oysters; sprinkle them; then another layer of cracker crumbs and oyster juice; then oysters, pepper, salt and butter, and so on, until the dish is full, the top layer to be cracker crumbs. Beat up an egg in a cup of milk, and turn over all. Cover the dish and set it in the oven for thirty or forty minutes. When baked through, uncover the top, set on the upper grate and brown.

OYSTER ROAST, NO. 2.

Put one quart of oysters in a basin with their own liquor, and let them boil three or four minutes; season with a little salt, pepper and a heaping spoonful of butter. Serve on buttered toast.

SALMON TURBOT.

One can of salmon, picked to pieces and all the bones removed. For the dressing, take one pint of cream and milk, mixed; put it on to boil, and when boiling add two small tablespoons of cornstarch, which has been mixed with a little cold milk. Cook ten minutes, stirring all the time, and add a little salt. Put a layer of salmon in a baking dish, then a layer of dressing, and so on until all is used. Sprinkle the top with bread crumbs and bits of butter, and bake fifteen or twenty minutes. Serve with slices of lemon.

MRS. JOHN BURCHARD.

FRIED OYSTERS.

Take large oysters from their own liquor into a thickly folded napkin, to dry them; then make hot an ounce of butter and lard, in a thick-bottom frying pan. Season the oysters with pepper and salt; then dip each one into egg and cracker crumbs rolled fine until it will take up no more. Place them in the hot grease and fry them a delicate brown, turning them on both sides by sliding a broad-bladed knife under them. Serve them crisp and hot. Some prefer to roll oysters in cornmeal, and others use flour; but they are much more crisp with egg and cracker crumbs.

MRS. A. J. CHAMBERLAIN.

MINCED CLAMS ON TOAST.

Open two dozen little neck clams and chop finely, taking care to save all the liquor. Put into a pan with half an ounce of butter, and season with red pepper and Worcester sauce. Stew for a few minutes and thicken with cream sauce. Serve on toast.

B. C. MORSE.

MOLDED SALMON.

Turn out a can of salmon and free the fish from skin and bones. Beat two eggs and add to the salmon, with one cup of bread crumbs, one tablespoon of lemon juice, one tablespoon of chopped parsley, and salt and pepper to taste. Pack in a well buttered mold and steam two hours.

MRS. J. L. WATSON.

CREAMED SALMON.

One pound salmon; one cup sweet cream; two teaspoons cornstarch, rubbed smooth with one tablespoon butter; one-half cup milk; a pinch of soda; pepper and salt to taste. Turn salmon from can to drain off liquor; pick fish into small flakes, carefully removing all bones and skin. Have ready the milk and cream, heated with soda, and add to them the cornstarch and butter, stirring constantly, until it thickens smoothly. Then put in salmon and toss about with fork until it is heated through. Remove from fire and turn into a greased baking dish. Sprinkle with bread crumbs and a few pieces of butter on top, and set in oven long enough to brown. Serve with sliced lemon, on toast or crackers.

SALMON.

One and a half pounds of fresh salmon, cut in one piece. Salt well and wrap in a thin cotton cloth; put in a steamer and steam until tender (about half an hour); carefully remove all skin and bones. Take a pint of sweet milk; let boil, and thicken with flour to a smooth gravy, adding a tablespoonful of butter, and salt to taste. Gently lay the salmon in it and let it heat through; then, carefully, so as not to break it into too small pieces, place it on a platter and turn the dressing over it. A pound can of salmon may be used in this way, removing the salmon from the can and taking away all bits of skin and bone and then heating it in the dressing.   MRS. LOUISA N. WIMER.

FRICASSEED OYSTERS.

Cook one pint of oysters in hot butter till plump, using one tablespoon of butter, half a saltspoon of white pepper, half a teaspoon of salt and a few grains of red pepper. Drain and keep them hot. Add enough cream to the liquor to make a large cupful. Cook one tablespoon of flour in one tablespoon of butter; add slowly the cream and oyster liquor, and a little lemon juice, if you like the flavor. Pour the sauce onto one well beaten egg; add the hot oysters and heat one minute. Serve on toast, if for breakfast; in paper cases, if for dinner or luncheon.

LOBSTER A LA NEWBURG.

One tablespoon butter; one tablespoon flour; one cup of cream; half cup of sherry wine; salt and red pepper to taste. Cook until thick Add meats of two good sized lobsters, or two cans of lobster. Serve hot on buttered toast.

B. C. MORSE.

SALMON CROQUETTES.

One can salmon, six rolled crackers, one egg, pinch of salt, one tablespoon cream or milk. Mash salmon fine; add egg, crackers and cream; form into rolls and fry in hot lard. This receipt will make one dozen.

MRS. MADISON.

POULTRY.

ROAST GOOSE.

Make dressing in usual manner; add to it three chopped apples and a large handful of prunes, not pitted. Stuff goose with this, and while baking baste often with wine and water, using wine alone for last basting. Remove grease, and add a little wine for gravy; thicken with flour. Currant jelly, lemon juice and hot water may be used instead of wine.

MRS. L. M. LANGE.

CHICKEN POT-PIE.

Cut up chicken; put into boiling water. When it boils, skim. Season and cook until tender. Thicken gravy a little. Make dumplings as follows: One pint flour, two teaspoons baking powder, one-half teaspoon salt, tablespoon sugar; mix, and wet with one small cup milk; roll one-half inch thick; cut in small pieces; put on top of chicken. Cook fifteen minutes.

CHICKEN PIE.

Make crust like baking powder biscuit, only a trifle shorter. Roll one-half inch thick, and line four-quart dish. Have ready two small chickens, which have been boiled till tender. Place pieces of chicken in pan; season. Put in pieces of butter; pour in liquor they were boiled in; roll crust for top; bake until crust is thoroughly done.

2

JELLIED CHICKEN.

Boil chicken until very tender; season with salt and pepper before removing from fire; let stock cool; then skim off oil and heat again. Stir in one tablespoon gelatine, which has been soaked one hour in three tablespoons of water. Slice two hard boiled eggs very thin, and place them around the sides and bottom of a dish. Cut chicken fine, leaving out skin, putting lightly in dish with eggs. Pour stock over this. When hardened, turn out on platter. Garnish with celery.

MRS. E. CHAMPLIN.

PRESSED CHICKEN.

Cut up the fowls, and place in a kettle with a tight cover to retain the steam, with two cups of water, salt and pepper to season, and lump of butter the size of an egg. Cook until the meat comes easily from the bones. Chop all fine, and pack in a mold, turning what juice remains over the chicken. When quite cold, slice, or simply turn out of the mold and serve. Do not let the water boil away while cooking.

MRS. J. L. GEE.

JELLIED CHICKEN.

Cook chicken and cut in pieces. Boil four eggs hard to each chicken; one box of Knox's gelatine, soaked in water. Season the liquor of the chicken. You should have about a quart. While hot pour over chicken. Place in a mold a layer of the meat, then a layer of the sliced egg, and so on. Then pour the liquor over.

MRS. JOHN L. WATSON.

BAKED CHICKEN.

Make nice dressing, stuff chicken, and roast until done, basting often with butter and water, if an open pan is used.

FRIED CHICKEN.

Cut up chicken; roll in flour, and then in beaten egg; have lard and little butter hot in iron spider. Put in chicken; salt and pepper; cover and cook until nicely browned; turn and brown other side. Veal cutlets are nice fried same way.

ROAST TURKEY.

Prepare your turkey by breaking the leg bones close to knee, pulling the tendons from the thigh. Pour over melted butter, and dredge with salt and flour. Stuff turkey. Put in a hot oven, and baste frequently, allowing fifteen minutes to the pound. When the legs begin to cleave from the body, it is done enough to remove from the oven.

DRESSING.

Take lean fresh pork and beef, equal quantities, and giblets of turkey. Put them in boiling water; cook until tender; then remove from stock, cool and chop fine. Return to stock, with some biscuit (either stale or fresh), with a piece of butter, salt and pepper, sage and onion for seasoning.

MRS. E. CHAMPLIN.

ROAST GOOSE.

Take a young goose; rub inside and out with salt.
Make stuffing with four common sized onions, one
ounce sage rubbed fine, one large coffee cup bread
crumbs and one of mashed potato, salt and pepper,
good piece butter, and an egg. Mix all together and
stuff goose. Do not fill too full. It will take two and
a half hours or more to cook it, with brisk fire. Baste
often, if open pan is used.

APPLE SAUCE TO SERVE WITH GOOSE.

Peel, core and cut up tart apples; stew them with
little water; add grated peel and juice of lemon;
sweeten to taste. When apples are done, mash smooth
and serve.

TURKEY DRESSED WITH OYSTERS.

For a ten-pound turkey, take one quart bread
crumbs, one-half cup butter (not melted), small teaspoon
each of pepper and salt, and one pint of oysters. Rub
turkey inside and out with salt; then fill first with
dressing, then a few oysters, with some of the liquor.
Cook giblets in dish, and chop fine for gravy. A fowl
of this size will require three hours' cooking in moderate oven.

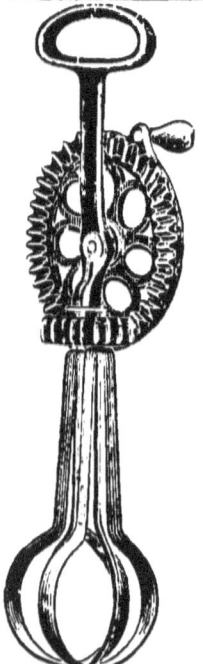

MEATS.

HOW LONG TO COOK.

Roast beef (weight eight pounds, rare)—Fifty minutes.

Roast beef (weight eight pounds, well done)—One and a quarter hours.

Ten minutes for each additional pound.

Twenty minutes longer for back of rump.

Saddle or loin of mutton—Same as beef, but for leg one and a quarter hours is the time.

Lamb—One and a half hours.

Veal—Three and three-quarter hours.

Pork—Three and a quarter hours.

Ham (boiled)—Six hours.

Ham (roasted)—Boil five hours, put in oven and roast two more.

MRS. L. S. SOWERS.

PRESSED MEAT.

Boil a soup bone thoroughly until meat drops off; pick off; season to taste with salt, pepper, a little sage if liked; press.

STEWED VEAL KIDNEY.

Boil kidney night before, until tender; turn meat and gravy in dish. In morning boil a few minutes; add little flour to thicken, a little onion, salt, pepper and lump butter. Serve on toast.

MRS. ROGERS

EGG AND MINCED MEAT.

Chop one pint cold chicken, ham or veal (or a little of each as you have on hand), and rub to a smooth paste. Add one tablespoon melted butter, one tablespoon chopped parsley, two beaten eggs, salt and pepper to taste. If too dry, moisten with little cream, stock, or gravy, but do not have it too soft to shape. Heat in a frying pan just enough to dry off. Form on a hot platter in a flat mound. Hollow the center, leaving a ridge around the edge. Keep hot, and put two or three poached eggs in center. Garnish with triangles of buttered toast around the edge; also, add a garnish of green parsley leaves.

MRS. JAMES BURCHARD.

MEAT BALLS.

Chop raw round steak, taking out all fat and gristle. Add pepper and salt, and work in with spoon one beaten egg, three tablespoons sweet cream. Work the whole with back of spoon until it forms a smooth paste. A little more cream or melted butter may be needed. Flour your hands lightly, make into balls, and fry in butter.

MRS. L. M. LANGE.

CHOPPED HAM.

Three tablespoons of ham, chopped fine; six eggs. Melt a large spoon of butter in a frying pan, drop the egg into it, and stir in the ham, which must, of course, have been previously cooked.

MRS. S. MARSHALL.

DRIED BEEF.

One-fourth pound of chipped dried beef pulled into shreds. Put in a skillet one tablespoon of butter and one of lard (or two of drippings). Add beef, and let fry until it curls up. Gradually add one heaping tablespoon of flour, and stir until well browned. Lastly, one pint of sweet milk is to be poured in, and gently stirred, so as to form a smooth gravy.

MRS. L. N. WIMER.

BAKED VEAL HAM.

Bone a breast of veal; chop the meat very fine; chop an equal quantity of cold boiled ham, and six cold boiled eggs. Butter a deep pan; put in a layer of veal; sprinkle with salt, pepper, thyme and anchovy or Worcestershire sauce, and then a layer of ham sprinkled with the egg. Fill dish with alternate layers, using both fat and lean of the ham; cover and bake slowly four hours. When done lay on it a weight. Serve in thin slices.

SELECTED.

JELLIED VEAL.

Boil veal tender; pick it up fine; put in a mold; add the water it was boiled in, and set in a cold place; season with salt and pepper to taste. A layer of hard boiled eggs improves it. Put eggs in bottom of pan that it is pressed in; soak one heaping teaspoon of gelatine in cold water, and add to the cup of liquor; pour over meat and eggs.

MRS. STANDRING.

SWEETBREAD CROQUETTES.

One pair of sweetbreads; one gill of milk; yolks of two eggs; five drops of onion juice; one-half table-spoon of melted butter; two tablespoons of flour; one tablespoon of chopped parsley; one-half teaspoon of salt; pepper and nutmeg to taste. Parboil the sweet-breads; chop them fine. Scald the milk, being careful not to scorch. Rub butter and flour together; stir into the milk. Take from the fire. Add the yolks of the eggs, sweetbreads and seasoning; salt to taste; mix well; turn out to cool; then form into croquettes. Dip each into the white of an egg, then in bread crumbs. Fry in hot cottolene. Nice served with green peas.

MRS. E. CHAMPLIN.

VEAL LOAF.

Three pounds of veal; half a pound of salt pork, chopped together; one cup bread or cracker crumbs; three eggs; one cup good stock; one lemon (juice and grated rind); one tablespoon chopped parsley and capers; pepper and salt to taste. Mix thoroughly, put layer of crumbs on top, and bake slowly for three hours. Serve with tomato sauce.

MRS. WM. EVERETT.

TOMATO SAUCE.

One quart can tomatoes; one onion, chopped fine; twelve cloves. Let all simmer for one hour. Rub through sieve; add salt, sugar and pepper to taste.

MRS. WM. EVERETT.

ROLLS OF COLD MEAT.

Take two cups of any cold cooked meat; mix with a tablespoon of butter, two tablespoons of bread crumbs, yolks of two eggs, one teaspoon onion juice, one of salt, half a grated nutmeg, a pinch of black pepper. Put in a frying pan over the fire; stir until heated. Take up. When cold, form in balls; dip first in beaten egg; then in bread crumbs; fry in cottolene. Serve with sauce made from stock: Melt one tablespoon butter and one of flour; mix one cup of stock and two tablespoons of cream; salt and pepper; stir until it boils; take from fire and stir in the beaten yolk of an egg.

MRS. E. CHAMPLIN.

POTTED BEEF.

Put beef in kettle with some little slices of salt pork at bottom, little salt and pepper. Pour over two tablespoons vinegar. When it has fried a little turn, and in ten minutes add one-half pint water. Don't let boil dry. Add little hot water occasionally. Cook slowly and keep covered. Is nice way to cook tough meat.

SELECTED.

MEAT ROLLY-POLY.

Chop fine the remains of a roast or steak; season with salt, pepper and a little nutmeg; also, a very little onion. Make a pie crust; roll thin, and spread thickly with the meat; roll it up and bake half an hour. Serve with brown sauce or tomato sauce.

MRS. WALTON.

VEAL CUTLETS.

A very nice way to cook cutlets and chops is to bake them. The great object is to have veal and mutton thoroughly done. By baking you best accomplish that object Take dripping pan; rub a little butter over each cutlet, salt and pepper, and lay flat in pans. Place in hot oven; cover with another pan same size. When done, make sauce called "Butter *Maitre d'Hotel:*" Rub to soft paste a small piece butter with flour; pour over one-half cup boiling water. It will then thicken. Then add one teaspoon of lemon juice. Pour over cutlets, and serve. Or, serve without sauce, if preferred.

CANNELON.

One pound uncooked beef, chopped fine; yolk of one egg; one tablespoon chopped parsley; one tablespoon butter; two sablespoons bread crumbs; one teaspoon lemon juice; one teaspoon salt; three dashes black pepper. Mix all together, and form into a roll about 6x4 inches. Wrap in greased paper and place in baking tin in a quick oven. Bake thirty minutes, basting twice with melted butter. Make a brown gravy, and pour around loaf, after placing it on a platter.

MRS. J. L. WATSON.

CREAMED HAM.

Warm one cup of finely chopped ham in one pint cream. Stir in quickly two well beaten eggs, little pepper and salt. Serve hot with thin slices of toast.

SELECTED.

SWEETBREAD.

Soak one pair of sweetbreads in cold salt water for an hour or two. Turn off the water, add more water and wash well. Parboil in salted water for fifteen or twenty minutes. Set away to get cold. Peel off the skin, cut in slices, and roll in egg and cracker crumbs. Fry in half lard and half butter.

MRS. JOHN L. WATSON.

SAUSAGE.

Five pounds chopped pork, lean and fat; five table-spoons salt; two tablespoons pepper; two tablespoons sage; two tablespoons summer savory. If you don't use summer savory, use more sage.

MRS. STANDRING.

BEEF LOAF.

One pound of chopped beef. Salt and pepper to taste. Two eggs; one-fourth loaf of bread soaked in sweet milk. Mix all thoroughly, and bake until brown.

FRANCES BLANCHE HILLYER.

VEGETABLES.

FRIED TOMATOES.

Take large green tomatoes; cut off both ends, then cut one in three slices. Have some butter in frying pan; let it get hot; roll tomatoes in flour; put them in pan; salt, pepper, and sprinkle little sugar on. Cook till they are nice brown, and you will have a nice dish.

SUCCOTASH.

Take one quart Lima beans, one-half pound salt pork, one and a half dozen ears sweet corn. Boil pork one and a half hours in three quarts water, putting in beans when pork has boiled one-half hour. Cut corn off, putting it in one dish; into another scrape milk from cobs. When the beans are nearly done, put in corn and boil fifteen minutes; then add the milk from cobs, boiling all ten minutes longer. It should be little thicker than gruel. Stir all the time after adding milk, or it will burn. If not sweet enough, add little sugar.

BOILED BAKED SWEET POTATOES.

Boil until tender; then slice several times the long way of potato. Place a layer in an earthen dish; sprinkle lightly with sugar, and heavily with butter; then another layer of potatoes, and so on, until dish is full, having butter and sugar for top layer. Bake thirty or forty minutes. MISS MARY HALSTED.

WARMED UP POTATOES WITH CREAM.

Use potatoes boiled in jackets; put butter in frying pan and let it get hot, but not burn; cut potatoes in small pieces; put them in pan with salt to taste. Let them cook thoroughly, stirring lightly to prevent burn- ing, but being careful not to mash or break the pieces. When ready to serve, pour over potatoes a quantity of thick, sweet cream, and stir them very lightly. Serve in hot dish.

MRS. C. E. PERSONS.

ASPARAGUS WITH CREAM DRESSING.

Tie the stalks in bunches, keeping heads one way, and cut the stalks of equal length; put them in well salted water, and cook until tender. Have ready thin slices of toast, and arrange the asparagus, when well drained, neatly upon it, and pour over it white sauce, made with one tablespoonful of melted butter and thickened with flour, in which is stirred one egg, two teacups of cream, with pepper and salt and all cooked until perfectly smooth.

ELIZABETH WALACE.

LADY CABBAGE.

Chop some cabbage very fine; cook in boiling water, one-half hour; drain, season highly with salt and pep- per, a half cup milk, and butter, size of an egg.

CARROTS IN CREAM.

Pare and slice carrots, stew in salt water for two hours, then pour cream, salt and pepper to taste.

POTATO PUFF.

Two cups cold, mashed potatoes; bits of some kind cold meat, hashed; two tablespoons melted butter; two well beaten eggs; one cup milk. Pour into deep dish and bake in quick oven. If rightly done, will merit its name.

BAKED SQUASH.

Cut in pieces; scrape well; bake from one to one and a half hours, according to the thickness of the squash. To be eaten with salt and butter, as sweet potatoes.

ENTREES.

CROQUETTES.

For every pint of meat, chopped fine (any kind of meat will do, but veal or chicken is the best), make a dressing of half a pint of milk, one large tablespoon of butter, two large tablespoons of flour, one tablespoon chopped parsley, one teaspoon onion juice, one teaspoon salt, half teaspoon grated nutmeg, cayenne pepper to taste. Put on to boil, and when boiling, add all the other ingredients previously mixed smooth in a little cold milk. Stir until thick, take from the stove and mix with the meat; let stand until cold. Form into croquettes; dip first in beaten egg, then in crumbs, and fry in boiling fat, the same as you would doughnuts.   MRS. H. M. BURCHARD.

RAMAKINS.

One-quarter pound grated cheese, one-quarter pound bread crumbs, salt and mustard to season, and the yolks of three eggs. Mix all these well together; make into small balls; dip in yolk of egg and fry until a pretty brown.   MRS. H. A. WELSFORD.

CORN OYSTERS.

One cup of grated corn (if you use canned corn, chop fine); half cup cracker crumbs; one egg, yolk and white beaten separately; add the white last; salt and pepper to taste. Fry in hot lard.

MRS. S. M. HARRINGTON.

A HUNGARIAN DISH.

Boil six eggs hard. When cold, peel and cut them in slices; then take five or six large potatoes; cut them in thin slices, as for frying, and place them in layers in buttered dish, commencing with potatoes, then egg, so on until the dish is full, leaving potatoes on top; add pepper, salt and butter to each layer; also, a very little sour cream, which will moisten the whole and give it a delicious flavor. Bake one and a half hours in moderate oven, and be careful not to burn on top.

MRS. H. A. WELSFORD.

MACARONI WITH CHEESE.

One-quarter pound, or twelve sticks macaroni, broken into one-inch lengths, and cooked in three pints boiling water; drain. Make a sauce of one tablespoonful each of butter and flour and one and one-half cups hot milk salt. Put a layer of grated cheese in bottom of bake dish, then a layer of macaroni and one of sauce, then cheese, macaroni and sauce, and cover the top with fine bread crumbs, with bits of butter dotted over, and a little grated cheese. Bake until brown.

EDITH ARVESEN.

CHEESE STRAWS.

One cup grated cheese; two tablespoons melted butter; three tablespoons cold water; salt to taste; add flour with a fork. Roll thin, like pie crust; cut one-half inch wide, and bake.

MRS. W. C. KAYSER.

DEVILED CHEESE.

Mix together three tablespoons grated cheese, one-half teaspoon salt, one-quarter teaspoon dry mustard, one teaspoon cream. dash of cayenne. Blend this with one heaping tablespoon butter. Spread over large, square crackers, and put in a hot oven until they begin to color.   MRS. J. L. WATSON.

CHEESE SANDWICHES.

Take one hard boiled egg; one-quarter pound cheese, grated; one-half teaspoon each salt, pepper and mustard; one tablespoon melted butter: one tablespoon vinegar or water. Take yolk, put in bowl and crumble it; put into it the butter. mix smooth with spoon; then add salt, pepper, etc.. mixing each well. Then put in vinegar. which will make proper thickness. Some would not like it so highly seasoned.

MIXED SANDWICHES.

Chop fine ham. tongues and chicken. For one pint meat use one-half cup melted butter. one tablespoon mustard. yolk of one egg. little pepper. Spread on thin bread and butter.

SARDINE AND HAM SANDWICHES.

Mince sardines fine, and mix with half the quantity cold boiled ham. minced fine. Spread over thinly sliced and slightly buttered bread.

CHEESE STRAWS.

To one cup of grated cheese add salt and pepper to taste, two tablespoons of melted butter, three tablespoons of cold water, and flour, to make a soft dough. Mix with a fork, until it no longer sticks to the sides of the bowl; lay upon a molding board dusted with flour; sift flour over the dough; roll gently, as thin pie crust; cut it in strips one-quarter of an inch wide, and bake.

MRS. EWING.

CORN OYSTERS.

Six ears of sweet corn (not too old). With a sharp knife split each row of the corn in the center of kernel lengthwise; scrape out all the pulp. Add one egg, well beaten; little salt; one tablespoon sweet milk; flour enough to make a pretty stiff batter; drop in hot lard, and fry a delicate brown. If corn is quite young, omit the milk, and use as little flour as possible.

SALTED ALMONDS.

Shell almonds; blanch by throwing in boiling water for few minutes; slip off skins, and spread them out to dry thoroughly. Put good piece butter in dripping pan; melt; stir almonds into it. Set in oven, stirring often until they begin to brown slightly. Take out and shake in colander to rid of grease. Sprinkle with fine, dry salt.

CHICKEN SANDWICHES.

Mince any cold chicken, boiled or roasted; put into sauce pan, with gravy, water, or cream, to soften it; add good piece butter; work very smooth while heating—most paste; put on plates to cool. Spread on buttered bread.

CORN OYSTERS.

One can of corn; three eggs; two teaspoons of baking powder; flour enough, so it will drop from a spoon; salt. Fry in hot lard.

MRS. F. WATSON.

SALADS.

SALAD DRESSING, WITH BUTTER.

Four tablespoons of butter; one of salt; one of sugar; one heaping teaspoon of mustard; a speck of red pepper; one cup milk; one-half cup vinegar; one tablespoon lemon juice; three eggs, beaten stiff. Let butter get hot in sauce pan; add flour, and stir until smooth, being careful not to brown. Add the milk, and boil up. Place the sauce pan in another of hot water; beat eggs, salt, pepper, sugar and mustard together; then vinegar; stir this into the boiling mixture and stir until it thickens. This will keep, when cold, about two weeks. B. C. MORSE, Chef Hotel Atlantic.

SALAD DRESSING.

Yolks of four eggs; two-thirds cup sugar; one tablespoon flour; one teaspoon mustard; one teaspoon salt; one cup vinegar; one tablespoon butter. Beat all but vinegar and butter until light; add them, and cook over water until smooth and thick. When ready to use, thin with sweet cream.

SALAD DRESSING.

Work yolks of two raw eggs smooth; add pinch salt and little cayenne pepper, one-half teaspoon dry mustard, one teaspoon olive oil or melted butter. Mix these ingredients thoroughly; add juice of half lemon. Keep adding melted butter until you have added one-half pint; add a few drops of lemon juice to every fifth teaspoon of butter until you have used two lemons.

MRS. L. M. LANGE.

CUCUMBER SALAD.

Two cucumbers, chopped; one onion, chopped; one-half dozen cold boiled potatoes, chopped; two bunches parsley, chopped; two tablespoons butter to one of vinegar, pepper and salt. Beat vinegar and butter with egg beater.   MRS. JOHN L. WATSON.

APPLE SALAD.

Cut celery and apples, and serve with dressing tied up in lettuce leaves.   MRS. O. E. JENKINS, Chicago.

CABBAGE SALAD.

Slice cabbage fine.

Dressing.—One egg, well beaten, stirred into one-half cup vinegar; a small lump butter; one teaspoon sugar; a trifle of mustard and salt. Place over fire, and stir until thick. If too strong, add little water. Cool, then pour over cabbage.   MRS. FISKE.

TOMATO ASPIC.

One-half box gelatine. Cover with one-half cup cold water. Take one pint cooked tomatoes (strained), one slice onion, one bay leaf, one-quarter teaspoon celery seed, one tablespoon lemon juice, little dash red pepper, one teaspoon salt. Bring to boiling point, and add gelatine. Strain at once, and put in molds. Stand away to harden. Serve on lettuce leaves with mayonnaise dressing.   MRS. C. H. WILLIAMS, Chatfield, Minn

FRUIT SALAD.

One pint gelatine dissolved in one pint cold water; add one pint boiling water; add four bananas, two pounds green grapes, one can pineapple (cut in small pieces) with juice, one-half pound candied cherries, four oranges (quartered), juice of two lemons, vanilla to flavor. A little sherry or claret is a great improvement; if used, put in less water. Place in mold, and let harden. May be served with or without whipped cream.   MRS. HARRY VAN TASSEL.

TOMATO SAUCE.

Take one can tomatoes. Put over the fire in stew pan. Add one slice onion, two whole cloves, a little salt and pepper. Boil twenty minutes, remove from fire, and strain through sieve. In another pan melt butter size of walnut. As it melts, sprinkle in one tablespoon of flour. Stir until it browns and froths a little. Into this stir the tomato pulp. Excellent for roast beef, and especially to pour over plain boiled macaroni or rice.
            MRS. L. A. WOODRUFF, Chatfield, Minn.

PREPARED MUSTARD.

Three teaspoons ground mustard; one teaspoon flour (two if the mustard is strong); one-half teaspoon sugar. Pour boiling water on these, and mix into thin, smooth paste. When cold, add vinegar to make ready for use Serve with salt.

MAYONNAISE DRESSING.

Two yolks of eggs, well beaten; one-half teaspoon mustard; one-half teaspoon salt; one and a half teaspoons vinegar; small one-half cup melted butter. Have all as cold as possible. Beat egg and mustard one minute. Begin adding butter, drop at a time, beating continually. When like jelly add little lemon juice, and begin adding few drops vinegar, beating well. If there is tendency to curdle, put on ice. When vinegar is used, add salt and pepper, whip five minutes and pour in glass dish and keep cool.

SALAD DRESSING.

Beat yolks of eight eggs; add one cup sugar, one tablespoon each salt, mustard and black pepper; one-half cup cream. Mix thoroughly. Bring to a boil one and a half pints vinegar; add one cup butter; let come to boil. Pour out mixture; stir well; bottle.

MRS. C. F. CASE.

SALAD DRESSING.

Yolks of two eggs; one teaspoon salt; two teaspoons sugar; one tablespoon butter; four tablespoons vinegar. Steam until thick, and when cold add one cup sweet cream.

MRS. J. B. GIBBONS.

NUT SALAD.

Three bunches celery; one pound English walnuts; one pound green grapes. Add chicken or any chopped meat, if desired.

MRS. H. M. LANGLAND.

SALAD.

Two bananas, sliced fine; equal amount of lettuce leaves, chopped not too fine; mix one cup sweet cream with two tablespoons of mayonnaise dressing. Mix all together lightly, and serve on lettuce leaves.

MRS. C. F. CASE.

TO PREPARE HORSERADISH FOR WINTER USE.

One coffee cup grated horseradish; two tablespoons white sugar; one-half teaspoon salt; one and a half pints vinegar. Bottle and seal.

CREAM SAUCE FOR FISH.

Heat one tablespoon butter in skillet. add one teaspoon flour, and stir smooth. Add one cup cold milk; let boil up once; season. Pour over boiled fish, salt or fresh.

SALAD DRESSING TO BE MADE AFTER SNOW PUDDING.

One-half cup vinegar; boil, and turn on the beaten five yolks; two teaspoons of salt, and one of pepper. Add mustard to taste, when used. Use about two tablespoons of this to one cup sweet cream, with little sugar added, for a pint of chopped cabbage.

MISS MINA E. ROSS, St. Charles, Minn.

EGGS.

OMELET.

Six eggs, whites and yolks beaten separately; one-half pint milk; six teaspoons cornstarch; one teaspoon baking powder; a little salt; add whites beaten to stiff froth. Cook in spider, with little butter in it. It is easily turned, if cut in four pieces. MRS. L. M. LANGE.

OMELET.

Take one egg for each person, beat two minutes; add salt and one tablespoon milk for each egg; beat one minute and turn into hot, well buttered frying pan. Cover it and cook slowly; raise edges and let soft part run under; cook until set; turn one-half over. Put onto hot platter, and serve at once. HOME GUIDE.

NICE WAY TO BOIL EGGS.

Put them on in cold water and let them just come to boil. If wished, soft-boiled are considered more digestible.

EGG BALLS.

Chop seven hard-boiled eggs; one dessert spoon chopped parsley; one heaping teaspoon grated cheese; two heaping teaspoons bread crumbs; one dessert spoon celery, and pepper and salt to taste. Mix together with three tablespoons mayonnaise dressing; roll in balls; dip in beaten eggs and bread crumbs, and fry in hot lard. Serve with cream sauce.

MRS. STANDRING.

There is but one

Flour.

It's everybody's favorite.

We all use it.

BREAD, BISCUIT, ETC.

ENGLISH SEED BREAD.

Take enough soft bread sponge to make a loaf of bread; add to it one-half cup sugar, not quite one-half cup butter and about one teaspoon caraway seed. Mix into a loaf and knead well. Let raise and bake.

MRS. J. P. WATSON.

BREAD OF WHOLE WHEAT FLOUR.

Take enough white soft sponge for number of loaves wanted, add little butter and sugar and enough whole wheat flour to enable to knead. Allow to rise in tine, then bake.

MRS. J. P. WATSON.

STEAMED BROWN BREAD.

One cup graham; one cup corn meal; one cup flour; two-thirds cup molasses; one cup sour milk; two cups sweet milk; one teaspoon soda; salt. Steam three hours in baking powder cans.

MRS. IDA HICKS.

SUPERIOR MUFFINS.

One cup sweet milk; three teaspoons sugar; one beaten egg, and butter one-half size of egg; two cups flour; one tablespoon baking powder. Beat quickly to a batter and bake in a quick oven, having the tins warmed in advance.

MRS. C. E. MEADER, Canton, Minn.

BROWN BREAD.

Two cups sour milk; two cups flour; two cups corn meal; one-half cup molasses; two small teaspoons soda. Steam two and a half hours.

MISS J. BOURSON.

GRAHAM BREAD.

Two eggs; two tablespoons butter; pinch salt; two tablespoons sugar; one pint buttermilk, sweetened with soda; one cup white flour; two cups graham flour; a little baking powder. Make batter quite stiff.

MRS. F. M. CUTTING, Delavan. Wis.

BUTTERMILK TEA CAKES.

One cup buttermilk, beaten to froth; one teaspoon (heaping) baking powder; one-half teaspoon soda; flour to make batter about the consistency of muffin batter. Bake quickly in gem pans and serve hot.

MRS. WINNIE DALE. Canton, Minn.

WAFFLES.

Two eggs, well beaten; pinch salt; one cup sour cream; two cups sweet milk; one teaspoon soda; one teaspoon baking powder; flour to make a stiff batter.

MRS. JOHN L. WATSON.

MUFFINS.

One glass milk; one glass whole wheat flour; one-half glass white flour; two tablespoons sugar; two tablespoons baking powder; salt.   MRS. HUMPHREY.

CORN BREAD.

Two cups Indian; one cup wheat;
One cup sour milk; one cup sweet;
One good egg that well you beat;
One-half cup molasses, too;
One-half cup sugar add thereto,
With one spoon butter, new,
Salt and soda each a teaspoon.
Mix up quick and bake it soon;
Then you'll have corn bread complete,
Best of all corn bread you meet.

MRS. H. R. WELSFORD.

SCOTCH SHORTBREAD.

Thoroughly dry one-half pound flour, into which mix six ounces of sifted sugar, a tiny pinch of salt, four ounces fresh butter and a teacup of cream. Mix well, and fill pretty little molds with the paste, which should be quite two inches thick. A pinch of cinnamon and a tablespoon of ground almonds are a great improvement. Bake for half an hour in quick oven.

MRS. H. R. WELSFORD.

QUICK GRAHAM BREAD.

One and a half pints sour milk; one-half cup molasses or brown sugar; two teaspoons soda dissolved in hot water, and as much graham flour as can be stirred in with a spoon. Pour into well greased pans, put in oven as soon as mixed, and bake two hours, or until done.

SELECTED.

4

WASHINGTON YEAST BREAD.

The yeast is easy to make, and, though liquid, keeps well, and is especially adapted to making bread in a cold climate or where no fire is kept over night.

YEAST.

Peel and boil two quarts of potatoes, mash fine and run through colander. Put in a two-gallon crock, and, while hot, add one small cup of flour, one even cup salt. Stir well, and add enough boiling water to fill the crock. When cool enough add two yeast cakes. If kept warm this will do to make bread next day, but is better if allowed to stand two days. Put away in cool place.

BREAD.

In morning take one quart of yeast, one quart water (or, if you want large baking, one and a half quarts), with flour enough to make stiff loaf. Add no salt, there being enough in the yeast. Set bread in warm place to raise. When light, mold in loaves. This makes six good sized loaves.

MRS. E. L. HEALY, Morris, Minn.

FRENCH ROLLS.

Into one pound flour rub two ounces butter and whites of three eggs, well beaten. Add two table-spoons good yeast, little salt, and milk enough to make a stiff dough. Cover, and set in warm place till light, which will be an hour or more, according to strength of yeast. Cut into rolls, dip into melted butter to keep from sticking together, and bake in quick oven.

SELECTED.

BOSTON BROWN BREAD.

The Bostonians, you know, are most cultured, 'tis said,
And it's greatly on account of their Boston brown
    bread.
The secret of making, I'm privileged to tell,
So, one cup of corn meal, dear sisters, scald well;
Then add to the same one cup of graham,
    And a cup and a half of white flour;
Of molasses a cup, and an egg beaten up,
    And one cup of milk that is sour;
One teaspoon and a half of soda to raise it,
And one of salt, or none would praise it;
Stir it up well, and four hours steam it;
And rest assured all will deem it
A greater treat than finest cake
That one could eat or cook could bake.

RAISED BISCUIT.

Two quarts flour; one quart milk or water; one cup
lard; one cup yeast; one tablespoon sugar; one tablespoon salt. Put half milk on lard; let scald; pour on
flour; mix all together; let rise; cut in biscuit; let
rise and bake.   MRS. PERMELEA PARKER.

ROLLS (GOOD).

One cup bread sponge; two cups scalded milk; six
tablespoons melted butter; one-half cup sugar; pinch
salt. Mix all into batter; let rise. Then make into
loaf; let rise again. Make into rolls, let rise and bake.

               MRS. BUMFORD.

TEA ROLLS.

For one dozen take one egg, two tablespoons lard, one tablespoon granulated sugar. This is to be added to the sponge, in the morning, that has been set over night. Mix up soft. Let it rise, then mix it down. When ready to put into pans, put it on bread board and roll it out; then cut with biscuit cutter, grease the top with lard, fold over and put into pans. Let rise again. When light, bake in a hot oven.

MRS. BAXTER WRIGHT.

POP-OVERS.

Three eggs well beaten; salt; one tablespoon melted butter; two and a half tablespoons sweet milk; one and a half cups flour. Beat very light. Bake about twenty minutes in quick oven.

MRS. WARD, Redwood Falls, Minn.

BREAKFAST TOAST.

To one egg well beaten add one cup sweet milk, two tablespoons of sugar. Slice bread and dip into the mixture till soaked through; then fry in hot butter till brown. Serve hot on hot platter.

MRS. A. DURENBERGER.

JOHNNY CAKE.

Two cups corn meal; one cup flour; one-half cup molasses; one teaspoon soda; little butter; salt; about one and a half cups sour milk. Beat up well and put in dripping pan.

MRS. P. J. CONSTANT, Brooklyn, N. Y.

GRAHAM BREAD.

Take the sponge of white bread, when light enough, for one or two loaves, as you like; add little sugar and shortening, and enough graham flour to make a stiff loaf. Place in pan, let rise, and bake in moderate oven.

SELECTED.

DROP BISCUIT.

One quart flour; three teaspoons baking powder; one small spoon salt; butter size of an egg, rubbed thoroughly in flour; one pint milk. Drop from spoon in buttered tins. Bake in quick oven.

SELECTED.

PUDDINGS.

EVE'S PUDDING.

If you want a good pudding, mind what you are taught;
Take eggs, six in number, when bought for a groat;
The fruit with which Eve her husband did cozen,
Well pared, and well chopped, at least half a dozen;
Six ounces of bread, let Moll eat the crust,
And crumble the rest as fine as the dust;
Six ounces of currants from the stem you must sort,
Lest you break out your teeth and spoil all the sport;
Six ounces of sugar won't make it too sweet;
Some salt and some nutmeg will make it complete;
Three hours let it boil without any flutter,
But Adam won't like it without wine and butter.

POOR MAN'S PUDDING.

One cup suet; one cup molasses; three cups flour;
three-quarters cup raisins, seeded; one egg; one-quarter cup currants; one teaspoon soda, dissolved in cup sweet milk; one-half teaspoon cinnamon; one-quarter teaspoon each cloves and allspice. Steam three hours and serve with liquid sauce.

MRS. B. C. MORSE, Hotel Atlantic.

ENGLISH PLUM PUDDING.

One pound raisins, seeded; one pound currants; one pound suet; one pound sugar; one pound flour; one-quarter pound citron; one teaspoon spices of all kinds; one cup milk, and six eggs. Steam six hours.

SNOW PUDDING.

Dissolve one-half package of Plymouth Rock phosphated gelatine in one-half cup cold water one hour; add one pint boiling water; stir until clear; add juice of one lemon and two cups sugar. Let cool until slightly thick, not solid. Beat whites of five eggs to stiff froth, turn gelatine on them very slowly, beating all the time, and continue to beat until it does not separate. Set on ice, and serve with whipped cream. Peaches may be halved and pressed into the mixture when almost solid, or it may be divided and another kind of fruit, as oranges, raspberries, pineapple, etc., be mixed with a part of it. A large dish is necessary for it.   MISS MINA ROSS, St. Charles, Minn.

ORANGE PUDDING.

Five oranges, peeled and sliced; add to these one cup of sugar, and let stand. Take one pint sweet milk, one tablespoon corn starch, and yolks of four eggs, well beaten. Boil together four minutes. Pour over oranges. Beat whites of eggs, add four tablespoons sugar, pour over pudding and put in oven to brown.   MRS. FRANK CUTTING. Delavan, Wis.

STEAMED PUDDING.

Three eggs well beaten; two and one-half tablespoons sugar; two tablespoons butter; three-fourths cup milk; one cup raisins, chopped; tablespoon baking powder; flour to make stiff as cake batter. Steam thirty-five minutes. Use cream and sugar sauce.

SELECTED.

BROWN CHARLOTTE PUDDING.

Butter pudding mold thickly and sprinkle butter with brown sugar. Cut thin slices of bread, butter them generously, then cut off crusts and line mold with them. Now fill mold with good baking apples, pared and sliced, with grated lemon peel and pieces of candied citron mixed throughout them. Sweeten with brown sugar. When mold is full, cover with thin slices of bread, dipped in melted butter. Bake for three hours in a moderate oven. When turned out it should be brown and crisp on the outside. Eat with cream.

MRS. HERBERT WELSFORD.

BREAD PUDDING.

One cup bread crumbs, soaked in a little hot water; three eggs, beaten light; two tablespoons sugar; butter size of walnut; one pint of milk; a few raisins and a teaspoon vanilla. Do not stir bread crumbs too much. Bake slowly. When done, spread first with jelly, cover with meringue made with the beaten whites of two eggs and two tablespoons sugar, and flavor with vanilla. Return to oven to brown slightly.

MRS. JOHN L. WATSON.

SUET PUDDING.

One heaping cup bread crumbs; two cups flour; one cup suet; one cup raisins; one cup molasses; one cup sweet milk; one tablespoon soda; one teaspoon salt; one teaspoon cinnamon; one cup finely chopped apple; little pinch ginger. Steam two hours.

MRS. ELLA WILCOX.

MOLASSES PUDDING (FINE).

One-half cup thick sour milk; two cups flour; one-half cup molasses; one-quarter cup butter; one teaspoon soda; one-quarter teaspoon cloves; one and a half cups raisins. Steam one hour, and serve with following

SAUCE.

One egg; one cup sugar, beaten well; one tablespoon butter. Beat and cook in dish of hot water. If too thick, add hot water.

MRS. FRANK CUTTING, Delavan, Wis.

ORANGE FLOAT.

Peel and slice four oranges; sprinkle over these one cup sugar and let them stand. Take one quart milk and one-half cup sugar; when boiling add two tablespoons cornstarch, which has been made smooth in the yolks of three eggs; cook till thick. Before removing from fire, flavor with vanilla. Let stand till cool, but not cold. Pour over sliced oranges. Whip whites of eggs to stiff froth with one-quarter cup of sugar. Wet a plate in cold water and place frosting on it; put in oven till it turns a light cream, then place on float.

MRS. CYRUS P. SHEPARD.

APPLE FRITTERS.

One cup sugar; one cup milk; one teaspoon baking powder; one tablespoon butter; four eggs; flour enough to make a thin batter. Cut apples in small pieces, dip in butter, and fry in lard.

MRS. E. M. LEWIS, Dawson, Minn.

DUTCH HUCKLEBERRY PUDDING.

Beat two eggs (not separately); add one tablespoon butter and one-half pint milk; sift one and one-half cups flour with one teaspoon baking powder; add it to eggs and milk. Pour into shallow greased tins, cover top thickly with huckleberries, sprinkle over one-half cup of sugar, and bake twenty minutes in hot oven.

ALMOND CREAM—BAVARIAN.

One and one-half pints cream; one pint blanched almonds; one-half box gelatine; three eggs; one cup sugar; one-half cup milk. Soak gelatine in milk two hours. Whip half the cream stiff. Put almonds and whipped cream on to cook with eggs and sugar. When the mixture begins to thicken, stir gelatine in and take from fire. Stir in whipped cream, flavor with vanilla, and place in mold. Serve when cold.

MRS. E. J. WAKEMAN.

PEACH DESSERT.

Pour one pint boiling water over one-half box gelatine; add two cups sugar, juice of two lemons; strain. When nearly cold, add the whites of two eggs, well beaten, and stir until it begins to jelly. Pare peaches, remove pits, and replace with chocolate creams; place peaches in glasses and pour over gelatine. Set on ice, and serve cold with whipped cream.

MRS. C. H. JOHNSON.

SUET PUDDING.

One cup suet, chopped fine; one cup sour milk; one cup molasses; one cup raisins, seeded and chopped; three and one-half cups flour; one teaspoon soda; one teaspoon cloves; little salt. Steam three hours.

VINEGAR SAUCE.

One cup boiling water; one cup sugar; one tablespoon flour; one tablespoon vinegar; a little nutmeg and salt. Mix flour with cold water, and stir into the boiling sugar and water. Then add vinegar and nutmeg. Cook twenty minutes.

MRS. J. W. BLAKE, Dalton, Ga.

RICE PUDDING.

One quart sweet milk; one rounding tablespoon rice; one teaspoon lemon and vanilla extracts mixed; one-half cup raisins. Sweeten to taste. Place in oven and stir often. Bake about two hours, or until rice is well done and pudding is consistency of custard. Serve warm or cold.

MRS. C. E. MEADER, Canton, Minn.

PRUNE WHIP.

Four tablespoons sugar; three-quarters pound prunes; whites of four eggs, beaten stiff. Stew prunes in as little water as possible until tender. Remove pits and rub pulp through sieve. Crack pits and wash the meats; mix with pulp; add this to the beaten whites of eggs and sugar. Bake twenty minutes, and serve with whipped cream.

MRS. F. C. WHITNEY.

FRIED CREAM.

One pint milk; five tablespoons sugar; butter size of hickory nut; yolks of three eggs; two tablespoons of cornstarch, and one of flour; one inch of stick cinnamon and a little vanilla. Put the cinnamon in the milk, and just before it boils stir in the sugar. Dissolve the cornstarch and flour in a little milk. Add this to boiling milk. Boil about two minutes; take from fire and stir in the beaten yolks; return to fire until it sets; remove from fire and take out the cinnamon; stir in the butter and vanilla. Pour on large platter and let cool. Later cut in pieces and shape desired; roll in cracker crumbs and beaten white of egg, then in cracker crumbs and let stand for a quarter or half an hour. Then fry in a wire basket in boiling lard.

MRS. T. A. WOODRUFF.

PRUNE PUDDING.

One dozen French prunes, cooked soft; take out pits and beat up fine; the whites of seven eggs beaten until light; one-half cup sugar sifted into eggs. Then add prunes, flavor with vanilla. Bake one hour in very moderate oven. To be eaten with whipped cream.

MRS. C. B. TYLER.

PEACH DUMPLINGS.

Make a crust as for apple dumplings; cut into square; roll in each a whole peach, adding a little butter and sugar to each dumpling. Put in pan and add a little water just before putting in oven. Eat with cream and sugar.

MRS. JOHN L. WATSON.

GRAHAM PUDDING.

Two cups graham flour; one cup molasses; one cup milk; one cup chopped raisins; one egg; one teaspoon soda, dissolved in little hot water; one-half teaspoon each ground cloves and cinnamon; a little nutmeg and salt. Steam three hours. Serve with following

SAUCE.

One cup sugar; one-half cup butter; two cups sweet milk, scalded cream, butter and sugar; add milk; just before serving, add well-beaten white of egg.

MRS. FREDENBURG.

BEST PUDDING.

One egg, beaten; three tablespoons sour cream that has been beaten; tablespoon molasses; scant half teaspoon soda; saltspoon salt; one-half cup chopped raisins or figs, and flour to make a very stiff batter. Or use any kind of fruit and omit molasses. Pour into buttered mold, set into cold water, and steam one hour. Serve warm, with cream and sugar, or a sauce made of one-half cup sugar, one tablespoon butter, one teaspoon flour, and one pint boiling water. Cook till smooth, and flavor.

MRS. SUSA FRICK.

SIMPLE DESSERT.

Dissolve one-half box Knox's gelatine in about one quart water; put on stove to heat; add one-half cup sugar and two tablespoons brandy (vanilla may be used). Pour over sliced peaches and serve cold with whipped cream spread on top.

MRS. EDITH ARVESEN.

COTTAGE PUDDING.

One cup sugar; two cups flour; nearly one cup cold water; one eg; butter size an egg; two teaspoons baking powder; salt. Bake in hot oven.

SAUCE.

One cup sugar; one-third cup butter; one table-spoon cornstarch. Mix and add two cups boiling water. After taking from stove, add juice of lemon.

CREAM PUFF PUDDING.

One cup boiling water, with half a cup butter melted into it. When this boils, stir in a cup of flour. Keep stirring until smooth and velvety; cool; add three eggs, well beaten, and one-quarter teaspoon soda, dry. Heat a pudding dish hot. Butter thoroughly and pour in the batter. Bake in a quick oven. Make an incision in the edge and pour in a custard made of one cup of milk, one-quarter cup flour, one-half cup sugar and two eggs; flavor with vanilla.

MRS. E. L. HILLYER, Minneapolis.

RICE PUDDING.

One cup rice; two quarts milk; five eggs; eight tablespoons sugar. Beat yolks of eggs and sugar together. After rice is cooked, add the milk, and when that boils, stir in the yolks and sugar. Beat the whites of eggs and five tablespoons sugar to a froth. Put this on as frosting and set in oven to brown. A cup of raisins may be added to pudding.

MRS. MATTIE A. HUGHES.

STEAMED PUDDING.

One-half cup butter, scant; two eggs, whites beaten separately and added last; two tablespoons sugar. Beat well together, then add one cup sweet milk and two cups flour, with two teaspoons baking powder sifted in; little salt. Slice peaches in bottom of cups; pour on batter. It will fill seven cups. Any fruit may be used. Steam one-half hour.

MRS. FRANK CUTTING, Delavan, Wis.

TAPIOCA WHIP.

One quart milk; one-half cup sugar (small); three tablespoons tapioca (large); three eggs; one tablespoon vanilla, or half lemon; three tablespoons powdered sugar. Soak tapioca in cold water three or four hours; then put tapioca and milk in double boiler and cook until tender; then add beaten yolks of eggs and sugar, cook slowly four or five minutes, flavor, stir in whites of eggs after they have been beaten with pulverized sugar, put in oven and brown.

MRS. NELLIE WARREN, Minneapolis.

PUDDING SAUCE.

One-half cup butter and one cup sugar, creamed as for cake; one pint water. Thicken with one tablespoon cornstarch, which has first been mixed with a little cold water. Let this mixture boil until thick, and remove from fire. When perfectly cold, mix with butter and sugar. This is especially nice for sweet pudding.

MRS. GEORGE LITTLE.

JAM PUDDING.

One-half cup sugar; one cup flour; one-half cup jam; one egg; two tablespoons butter; three tablespoons sour milk; one small teaspoon soda; one-half teaspoon spices. Make like a cake, and bake.

JELLY FOR THE CAKE OR PUDDING.

One-half cup sugar; one-half cup water; yolks of two eggs; a large tablespoon of flour; a little butter; juice and rind of one lemon. Cook, and when pudding is done spread this on top, and beat the whites of two eggs to a stiff froth, with one spoonful of sugar spread on top, and put in oven to brown. Eat with sauce.

MRS. STANDRING.

FRUIT FLOAT.

The whites of three eggs, beaten to stiff froth; six tablespoons powdered sugar. Beat five minutes; add three tablespoons jelly, and when well incorporated set away in cool place. Serve with following

SAUCE.

Yolks three eggs; two tablespoons sugar. Heat milk in double boiler, add eggs and sugar. Cook till like cream. To be eaten cold.

MRS. J. GOODWIN.

CREAM PUDDING.

Stir together one pint of sweet cream, one-half cup of sugar, the yolks of three eggs, a little nutmeg; then add the whites well beaten, stir, and pour into a buttered pieplate and sprinkle bread crumbs to about an inch thick; then bake.

MRS. A. DURENBERGER.

5

BLACKBERRY PUDDING.

One and one-half pints sifted flour; sprinkle a little of it over one pint or more of fresh blackberries. Take one-half cup sweet milk and dissolve in it an even teaspoon of soda, then nearly fill with molasses. Stir in flour until you have a smooth batter, and lastly add the berries, stirring lightly, not to break. Steam until done.

SAUCE.

One cup sugar; one-half cup butter, creamed. Put one-half cup water in saucepan, and heat. Thicken slightly with flour, and stir in rapidly the butter and sugar. Flavor with vanilla or any preferred flavoring.

MRS. BUCKMEN, Waseca, Minn.

BIRDIE'S BANANA SHORTCAKE.

One pint of flour; one large teaspoon of baking powder; one-third cup shortening, made moist with milk. Take three bananas and some orange juice; grate the yellow rind from orange and mix with sugar. Slice the bananas, split the cake, butter, and fill with the prepared fruit; add a spoonful of cream or the white of an egg, beaten. First cousin to strawberry shortcake.

BIRDIE CHAMPLIN.

PUDDING SAUCE.

One cup pulverized sugar; butter size of egg. Beat first yolks, and mix with butter and sugar; then add beaten whites and beat all thoroughly.

MRS. ANNIE C. WARD.

CHOCOLATE BAVARIAN CREAM.

One pint sweet cream, whipped stiff; one cup milk; one-half cup sugar; one-half box gelatine; one square chocolate grated fine; add two tablespoons sugar and one tablespoon of water. Stir over fire until smooth and glossy. Have the remaining half cup of milk boiling; stir chocolate and gelatine in the milk. When cool, add whipped cream. Flavor with vanilla. Place in mold and serve when cold.　MRS. E. J. WAKEMAN.

EGG SAUCE FOR SWEET OR COTTAGE PUDDING.

Two eggs, beaten separately; to the yolks add a scant cup of sugar, and beat very light; to this add three tablespoons boiling water (no more); flavor as desired. Beat the whites stiff, and add just before serving.　MRS. C. H. WILLIAMS.

APPLE FRITTERS.

Mix the yolks of two eggs with one tablespoon sugar; add one cup warm sweet milk and two cups flour, having sifted one heaping teaspoon of baking powder through it; stir in beaten whites of two eggs and sour apples, pared and very thinly sliced. Drop from spoon into hot lard, and fry light brown. Same sauce as for blackberry pudding or any good liquid sauce.
MRS. BUCKMEN, Waseca, Minn.

PUDDING SAUCES.

One cup sugar; one cup water; yolks of three eggs; butter size of egg; two tablespoons cornstarch. Boil until thick, and add the beaten whites of the eggs.
MISS ALICE C. STEWART.

HELP WANTED.

here is a constant and growing demand

for competent girls for general housework in Marshall. All such can be given excellent places at good wages.

The Editorial Committee of this book invites correspondence from reliable girls who wish to secure work here, and will be pleased to confer with Marshall ladies who desire to employ such help:

MRS. WM. ROGERS,

MRS. F. M. HEALY,

MRS. C. M. BOUTELLE,

MRS. J. W. WILLIAMS,

EDITORIAL COMMITTEE.

MARSHALL, MINN.

PIES.

CREAM PIE.

One coffee cup cream and milk; one tablespoon flour; yolks of two eggs; one-half cup sugar. Put this in crust, and bake. After taking from oven, spread lightly with grape jelly. Add meringue made of whites of two eggs and two tablespoons sugar. Return to oven and brown.

MRS. J. G. SHUTZ.

COCOANUT PIE.

One pint milk; one cup sugar; three eggs; one cup cocoanut. Mix the yolks of the eggs and sugar together; stir in the milk and cocoanut; bake with one crust. When done, beat whites of eggs to a froth, stirring in two tablespoons powdered sugar; pour over pie; return to oven and brown lightly.

MRS. E. L. NESBITT, Brooklyn, N. Y.

LEMON PIE.

One cup sugar; juice of one lemon; one cup hot water; two spoons cornstarch; two eggs. Boil half of sugar with water. Mix yolks of eggs, cornstarch and the other half cup of sugar. Stir into boiling syrup; cook five minutes; add about a tablespoon of butter. Have shell baked crisp; turn in the jelly; beat whites with two dessert spoons of sugar, and pour over. Brown lightly. If used the same day made, it is delicious.

MISS MINA ROSS, St. Charles, Minn.

CHOCOLATE PIE.

Two tablespoons Baker's (or sweet) chocolate; two heaping teaspoons cornstarch; one cup sweet milk; one cup sugar; yolks of three eggs, reserving the whites for frosting. Cook the milk, chocolate, eggs, etc., until you think sufficient; then fill in crust, which has been baked previously; frost and brown.

MRS. A. P. BAKER.

LEMON PIE.

One lemon, grated and squeezed; yolks of four eggs; one tablespoon butter; one and a half cups of white sugar; two and a half tablespoons of flour in one cup of warm water (boil and pour in with other before cooling). Put in crust, and bake. Use the whites for frosting.

MRS. F. M. CUTTING, Delavan, Wis.

PINEAPPLE PIE.

One cup sugar; one-half cup butter; one cup sweet cream; five eggs. Add the beaten yolks of eggs, then the pineapple and cream, and lastly the beaten whites, whipped lightly. Bake with an under-crust only.

MRS. WM. THORBURN.

GETTYSBURG MOCK MINCE PIE.

One cup chopped raisins; one cup currants; one cup thick sour milk; one cup sugar; salt and spice to suit taste (allspice preferred); small piece of butter; two eggs.

LEMON PIE.

Line a deep pie tin with good crust. Yolks of four eggs, beaten smooth; add two-thirds cup granulated sugar. Beat. One cup sweet cream; tiny pinch of salt; rind and juice of one lemon added the last thing. Bake.

MERINGUE.

Whites of four eggs, beaten stiff; four teaspoons granulated sugar. Spread on the pie, return to the oven, and brown with a slow fire.

MRS. JAS. ELLS, Minneapolis, Minn.

MINCE MEAT.

Five pounds of beef, chopped fine; four pounds suet; five pounds raisins, seeded; five pounds brown sugar; one pound citron; eight oyster crackers; two lemons, chopped fine; two pints cider; one quart molasses; one quart cherry wine; one quart brandy; one gill rose water; one quince, chopped fine; one tablespoon salt; eight tablespoons cloves; thirteen tablespoons cinnamon; four teaspoons mace; one nutmeg. Mix molasses, crackers, cider, wine, brandy and spices. Add twice the amount of apples to meat.

B. C. MORSE. Hotel Atlantic.

PIE CRUST.

One cup flour; one salt spoon salt; one-half cup lard. Mix with as little ice water as you can to roll out.

MRS. JAS. ELLS, Minneapolis, Minn.

PIE-PLANT PIE.

Two eggs; one tablespoon flour; one teacup sugar; small lump butter. Beat well together. Add the pie-plant cut fine; beat well together, and bake with two crusts.

MRS. JOS. BROWN.

RHUBARB MINCE PIE.

Three cups chopped rhubarb; one cup molasses; one cup sugar; one cup butter; one cup water; one cup chopped raisins; five crackers (pounded); pinch salt; even teaspoon each of cloves, allspice, cinnamon. This will make three pies.

MRS. WILCOX.

APPLE PIE.

Peel and grate four large tart apples, or one cup; one-half cup water; one-half cup sugar; little butter; cinnamon or nutmeg. Bake in one crust. Use the whites of two eggs, beaten stiff, or whipped cream for the top, and brown in oven.

MRS. JOHN L. WATSON.

LEMON PIE.

Juice one lemon and one-half the rind, grated; two eggs, beaten; two tablespoons flour, mixed with one cup sugar; one small cup water. Pour this into pie tin lined with rich paste, and bake till filling is well set. Frost with whites of two eggs, beaten stiff, and bit of sugar added. Lightly brown over, and serve cold.

MRS. C. E. MEADER.

MINCE MEAT.

I get five pounds lean beef, without bone (which will make three and a half quarts finely chopped beef), fifteen quarts chopped apples, eight quarts sweet cider, two quarts boiled cider, four pounds raisins (seeded), three pounds currants, one and a half pounds citron, one-half pound lemon peel, one and a half pounds chopped suet, two cups New Orleans molasses, four cups butter, six teaspoons mace, eight teaspoons cinnamon, five teaspoons each of cloves and allspice, and light brown sugar. Boil four or five hours, stirring often to prevent burning. This makes a large quantity, but will keep nicely, and should there be any left in spring, it can be boiled up, put into fruit jars, and be all right for another year.

MRS. WM. EVERETT, Waseca, Minn.

CURRANT CREAM PIE.

One cup currants; one cup sugar; one cup milk; two heaping tablespoons flour in the sugar. Stir sugar and milk until dissolved. Add currants last (do not crush). Made with one crust.

MRS. JOHN L. WATSON.

CRANBERRY PIE.

One heaping cup cranberries; one tablespoon flour, mixed with one cup sugar; one-half cup water. Bake with two crusts in moderate oven.

MRS. JOHN L. WATSON.

FILLING FOR CREAM PIE WITH TWO CRUSTS.

One pint sweet cream; one egg, beaten; five table-spoons sugar; one tablespoon flour; one-half teaspoon lemon extract. Bake with two crusts, and serve cold.

MRS. C. E. MEADER.

CURRANT PIE.

Bake the crust first; then to as many currants as is required for one pie add one cup sugar, one tablespoon flour, yolks of two eggs. Mix well and cook. When thick remove from the stove and pour into the baked crust, and frost with the whites of two eggs. Set in oven and brown.   MRS. CORA CUTTING.

CRANBERRY PIE—FINE.

One and a half cups mashed cranberries; one-half cup raisins. Mix one tablespoon flour with one cup sugar. Stir this in with the cranberries, then add one-half cup cold water. Put on the stove, and cook until the cranberries are done. Cool, pour into the crust, and cover the top with a crust. Bake.

MRS. CORA CUTTING.

PUMPKIN PIE.

Two cups stewed pumpkin; pinch of salt; one egg; two-thirds cup sugar; one-half teaspoon ginger; one teaspoon cinnamon; one-half teaspoon cloves; one scant pint of milk. This makes one large pie.

MRS. CUTTING.

CREAM PIE.

Line a pie tin with rich crust. Place a cup of milk on the stove, with one-half cup sugar. When hot, thicken with a large tablespoon of cornstarch. Then take from stove, and add the white of one egg, beaten to a stiff froth, and a teaspoon of vanilla extract. When cool whip about one-half cup of sweet cream, flavored, and spread over the pie.

MRS. J. STURGEON.

APPLE PIE.

Pare and slice thinly three or four apples; spread over crust; sweeten to taste; then add a large tablespoon of vinegar, and four or five pieces of butter, size of a hazelnut. Add top crust, and bake brown.

MRS. A. DURRENBERGER.

CREAM PIE.

Stir a pint of sweet cream with a cup and a half of powdered sugar. Let stand while beating the whites of three eggs. Mix together thoroughly. Use nutmeg or vanilla for flavor. This will make a large pie, or two small ones without upper crusts.

MRS. A. DURRENBERGER.

TOMATO PIE.

Peel and slice green tomatoes. Add two tablespoons vinegar, small piece butter, three tablespoons sugar and a little nutmeg. Bake with two crusts, slowly.

ENGLISH MINCE MEAT.

In making mince meat, each ingredient should be minced separately and finely before adding to the others. Take two pounds stoned raisins, two pounds currants, two pounds beef suet, one pound apples (pared and cored), two pounds brown sugar, one-half pound candied orange peel, one-quarter pound citron, grated rind of three lemons, one grated nutmeg, one-half ounce salt and one teaspoon ginger. Mince well, and add half pint French brandy. Press it into jars, and tie down.   MRS. WELSFORD.

MINCE MEAT.

Three bowls meat; five bowls apples; one bowl molasses; one of vinegar; one of cider; one of suet or butter; two of raisins (seeded); five of sugar (light brown); one bottle of brandy (or, if you prefer, leave out brandy and add more cider); one tablespoon each cinnamon and cloves, one tablespoon each salt and black pepper; juice and grated rind of three lemons. Add all but meat and spices; boil until raisins are tender; pour onto meat and spices. Add brandy after it is cold. If suet is used, scald it. I use bowl which holds little more than quart.   MRS. ROGERS.

PIE CRUST.

Three tablespoons flour; one of lard; two of water; little salt. Will make sufficient for one crust, and no waste.   MRS. JAMES BURCHARD.

MINCE MEAT.

For every cup of cooked chopped meat, take two cups chopped apples, one cup meat broth or liquor, one cup raisins, one cup currants, one cup brown sugar, one-half cup molasses, one teaspoon cinnamon, one-half spoon each allspice and cloves, one-quarter teaspoon mace, the juice and grated rind of one lemon, one-quarter pound citron, one-half pound candied fruit. Mix well togther, and add one cup sweet pickle vinegar and all remnants of jelly and preserves.

MRS. BUMFORD.

CUSTARD PIE.

Use tin one and a half inches dep. Line with crust, and set on stove for a minute to cook crust. Heat nearly a quart of new milk to boiling. Beat two eggs with three large tablespoons sugar. Flavor to taste, pour hot milk on, turn in crust, and bake just long enough to be firm. If some cream is used it is an improvement. The queen of custard pies.

MRS. ROGERS.

CAKE.

SPONGE CAKE.

Beat together yolks of four eggs and two cups of pulverized sugar; stir in gradually one cup of sifted flour and the whites of four eggs, beaten to a stiff froth; then a cup of sifted flour, in which two teaspoons of baking powder have been stirred, and lastly a scant teacup of boiling water, stirred in a little at a time; pinch salt; flavor. Do not make it any thicker. Bake in shallow pans.   MRS. CYRUS P. SHEPHERD.

SPONGE CAKE.

Three eggs; one coffee cup flour; one cup sugar; one rounded spoon baking powder; two tablespoons sweet cream; one teaspoon vanilla. Put all the ingredients in the dish together, and stir briskly ten minutes. Bake in quick oven.   MRS. E. FRENCH.

SNOW CAKE.

One-half cup butter; one cup sugar; one and a half cups flour; one-half cup milk; whites of four eggs; one teaspoon baking powder. To be baked either in loaf or layers.

PLAIN CAKE.

One cup sugar, one cup sweet milk, one egg or the whites of two, butter size of walnut, two teaspoons baking powder, two cups flour. Flavor with lemon.

.   MRS. W. MAXSON.

SPONGE CAKE (AFTER MAKING ANGEL'S FOOD).

Yolks of eleven eggs; one cup sugar; one and a half cups flour; one-half cup boiling water; one teaspoon baking powder.   MISS MINA ROSS, St. Charles, Minn.

FRUIT CAKE.

One pound of raisins, seeded; one pound of currants; one-half pound citron; two cups brown sugar; three cups flour; one cup butter; four eggs; one-quarter cup each coffee and brandy; one teaspoon soda; one teaspoon cinnamon, less of cloves and allspice; a few chopped nuts; one nutmeg.   MRS. WAKEMAN.

HOME FRUIT CAKE.

Three teacups flour, sifted, with three teaspoons baking powder; one teacup each brown sugar and molasses; one-half cup butter; three eggs; one-half teaspoon each allspice, cloves, cinnamon and nutmeg; one-half pound each stoned raisins, currants, figs and citron, cut fine; one teacup chopped nut meats. Mix fruit and spices the day before making cake. Bake in slow oven.   MRS. W. H. SIMONS, Morris, Minn.

WALNUT CAKE.

One and a half cups sugar; one-half cup butter; two cups flour; whites of four eggs; small three-quarters cup of sweet milk; two teaspoons baking powder; one cup walnut meats, chopped.   EDITH ARVESEN.

SCRIPTURE CAKE.

One cup butter.........................Judges v., 25.
Three cups flour.....................I. Kings iv., 22.
Two cups sugar.......................Jer. vi., 20.
Two cups raisins.................I. Sam. xxx., 12.
Two cups figs.......................I. Sam. xxx., 12.
One cup water.........................Gen. xxiv., 17.
One cup almonds....................Gen. xliii., 11.
Six eggs...............................Isa. x., 14.
One tablespoon honey (large).........Exodus xvi., 31.
Pinch of salt.........................Lev. ii., 13.
Spices to taste......................I. Kings x., 10.
Two tablespoons baking powder.........I. Cor. v., 6.

Follow Solomon's advice for making good boys, and you will have a good cake (Proverbs xxiii., 14).

MRS. E. L. HEALY, Morris, Minn.

POOR MAN'S FRUIT CAKE.

One cup shaved maple sugar; one cup sour milk; two cups flour; one cup raisins; two tablespoons molasses; five tablespoons butter; one teaspoon soda; one teaspoon each cinnamon, cloves and allspice; one-half cup almonds. MRS. MARTHA TOWN, Black River, N. Y.

EVERYDAY FRUIT CAKE.

Two eggs; one cup brown sugar; one-half cup butter; one-half cup sour milk; one cup raisins, seeded and chopped; one and a half cups flour; one teaspoon soda; mixed spices and flavoring to taste. One loaf, simple and cheap. MRS. W. M. ROSS, St. Charles, Minn.

6

PORK FRUIT CAKE.

Two cups salt pork, chopped; two cups boiling water; two cups sugar; one cup molasses; one pound raisins; one pound currants; one-half pound citron; three teaspoons baking powder; flour to make as other fruit cake; spices to taste. Bake two hours.

MRS. WILL ROGERS.

WHITE FRUIT CAKE.

One cup butter; two cups sugar; one cup sweet milk; two and a half cups flour; whites of seven eggs; two even teaspoons baking powder; one pound each seeded raisins, almonds, figs, and one-fourth pound citron. Bake two hours.

FRUIT CAKE.

One pint sugar; one quart flour; one cup butter; one cup sweet milk; four eggs; one pound each currants and citron; two pounds raisins; one teaspoon each mace, cinnamon and cloves; one teaspoon soda; one and a half wineglasses brandy.

MRS. F. P. WILLARD, Russell, Minn.

CLOVE CAKE.

Four cups flour; two cups sugar; one cup butter; two eggs; one cup sweet milk; one pound raisins; one teaspoon soda: one teaspoon ground cloves; one tablespoon each cinnamon and nutmeg. This cake will keep fresh for several weeks.   MISS ANNA PEARCE.

FRUIT CAKE.

One pint butter; two pints brown sugar; one pint flour; one cup dark molasses; ten eggs; six cups raisins; three cups citron; three cups almonds, after they are blanched; three cups currants; three cups figs; one teaspoon each, cinnamon, cloves, allspice and nutmeg; one gill brandy and one gill sherry wine. Stone the raisins. Wash and dry thoroughly the currants. Shred the citron. Cut figs in small pieces. Put all together in wooden bowl, and chop fine. Chop and add the almonds, then sprinkle and rub thoroughly with an extra pint flour, which has been browned. The cake is lightly put together in the usual way, and the fruit put in last. Line pans with thick buttered paper, and bake slowly in a moderate oven.

MRS. C. F. CASE.

FIVE-MINUTE CAKE.

One cup sugar; one-quarter cup butter; one-half cup cold water; one and a half cups flour; one and a half teaspoons baking powder; whites of two eggs. Put together in dish, and stir five minutes. Bake in small pan, and use any frosting.

MRS. MARTHA TOWN, Black River, N. Y.

CORNSTARCH CAKE.

One-half cup butter; one and a half cups sugar; one cup cornstarch; one and a half cups flour; one cup milk; one teaspoon baking powder; whites of four eggs beaten to a stiff froth; flavor to taste.

MRS. JOHN STRUTHERS, Faribault, Minn.

DEVIL'S CAKE.

One cup sugar; one-half cup butter; one-half cup sweet milk; two eggs; two and a half cups flour; one teaspoon soda dissolved in hot water.

Chocolate Part.—Put over fire one cup sweet milk; one cup grated chocolate. Stir until dissolved, then stir into it one cup sugar and the yolk of one egg which has been beaten light. Cook until thick. When cool mix custard with cake, and bake in layers. Put together with white frosting.　　MRS. NEWMAN.

DARK FIG CAKE.

Two cups sugar; one cup butter; one cup water, with one teaspoon soda dissolved into it; three cups raisins, chopped fine; one teaspoon cinnamon; a little nutmeg; four eggs; flour to make as stiff as pound cake. Take one pound figs, put a thin layer of cake in two tins, divide the figs, and cover batter with them. Bake remainder of batter, and cover the figs. Put two cakes together, with icing.

MRS. W. B. THORBURN.

BIRTHDAY CAKE.

One cup butter; two cups sugar; three cups flour; one cup milk; four eggs; two teaspoons baking powder. Bake in large dripping pan, and frost heavily. When frosting is partly dry, mark off in squares, and put half an English walnut meat on each square. A very nice cake.

MRS. EDWARD LAMM, Watertown, S. D.

LINCOLN CAKE.

Rub one pound sugar and three-quarters pound butter together; add beaten yolks of six eggs, two cupfuls sour cream, with one teaspoon soda, dissolved in a little boiling water, and stirred into it just before adding to the cake; one teaspoon each nutmeg and cinnamon; one pound sifted flour; one tablespoon rosewater; one-half pound citron, cut fine; and lastly, the whites of six eggs, beaten stiff. Beat all together, and bake in square pans.

MRS. ROGERS.

SPICE CAKE.

One cup brown sugar; one cup white sugar; one cup butter; one cup cold coffee; one tablespoon each vanilla and allspice; one-half teaspoon cinnamon; yolks of eleven eggs; flour to make a batter (not too stiff).

MRS. C. F. CASE.

ANGEL'S FOOD.

One tumbler of flour, sifted five times; one tumbler of sugar, sifted three times; one teaspoon cream tartar; pinch salt; one teaspoon vanilla; whites of eleven eggs, well beaten. Sift cream tartar into flour the last time. Bake forty minutes in moderate oven.

MRS. F. M. CUTTING, Delavan, Wis.

GINGER CAKE.

One egg, well beaten; one cup molasses, beaten well together; add two-thirds cup boiling water poured onto one-half teaspoon soda; one-and a half cups flour; one-half teaspoon ginger, and good four tablespoons melted butter. Bake in moderate oven.

MRS. CUTTING.

ANGEL'S FOOD CAKE.

Take the whites of nine or ten eggs, according to size, and add pinch salt. When partly whipped, add one dessert spoon of lemon juice (not extract). When thoroughly whipped, add one cup granulated sugar and one teaspoon vanilla. Sift one cup flour three or four times, and stir carefully into cake. Bake forty-five minutes.   HAZEL WAKEMAN.

CHOCOLATE CAKE.

Three eggs; one cup sugar; one cup sour milk; one-half cup butter; one-half teaspoon soda; one teaspoon vanilla; one-quarter bar Baker's chocolate; one good cup flour.

ICING.

Four tablespoons sweet milk; stir stiff enough to spread with powdered sugar.
                    MRS. SPEAR, Lake Crystal, S. D.

CARAMEL CAKE.

One cup sugar; one-half cup butter; one-half cup sweet milk; two eggs; two and one-half cups flour; one teaspoon soda dissolved in hot water. Put on the stove one cup sweet milk, one cup Baker's chocolate, grated. Stir until dissolved. Then stir into it one cup sugar and the yolk of one egg, which has been beaten lightly. Mix all together, and when cool mix custard with cake, and bake in three layers. Put together with jelly to give a tart taste.
                    ANNIE E. WARD, Redwood Falls.

BREAKFAST FRUIT CAKES.

One cup light brown sugar; one-half cup butter; one cup thick, sour cream; two eggs, well beaten; two cups flour; one large cup raisins; one teaspoon soda; one level teaspoon cloves; two level teaspoons cinnamon. Bake in iron gem pans, and serve with coffee. Can be used for loaf cake also.

MRS. BESSIE MEADER, Canton, Minn.

WASHINGTON PIE.

Two eggs; One cup sugar; one-half cup milk; one tablespoon butter; one and one-half cups flour; one teaspoon baking powder. Bake in layers.

CREAM FOR FILLING.

One-half pint milk; one egg; one-half cup sugar; two teaspoons cornstarch; small piece butter. Flavor with vanilla. Cover top of cake with whipped cream.

MRS. HUMPHREY.

CREAM PUFFS.

Boil with large cup hot water one-half cup butter. Stir in one cup flour. Let cook until it cleaves from side of dish. Set aside to cool. When cold, stir in four eggs, one at a time, without beating. Drop on buttered tins, and bake in fairly hot oven.

CREAM FOR FILLING.

One-half pint milk. Let come to boil. Stir in one egg, one-half cup sugar, two tablespoons flour, which have been mixed together. Flavor to taste.

MRS. PAIGE.

ROLLED JELLY CAKE.

Four eggs; beat yolks. Add one cup sugar and beat again. Add one tablespoon water, one cup flour sifted with one teaspoon baking powder, and, lastly, add whites of four eggs, beaten to stiff froth. Line pan with thin brown paper. Do not butter either pan or paper. When done, let cool a little, and turn cake out. Wet cloth in cool water, brush over paper and pull off. Spread cake with jelly, roll up, and sprinkle with powdered sugar.   MRS. NEWMAN.

CARAMEL CAKE.

One-half cup butter; one-half cup sugar; two cups flour; nearly one cup sweet milk; even teaspoon baking powder; teaspoon flavoring; whites of four eggs. Bake in small dripping pan or in layers.

CARAMEL.

Two cups brown sugar; one-half cup sweet cream; one tablespoon butter. Cook until thick, then add one teaspoon vanilla.   MRS. J. E. ELLS, Minneapolis.

DARK LAYER CAKE.

One cup molasses; one cup sour cream; one-half cup butter; two cups flour; two level teaspoons soda; two teaspoons cinnamon; one teaspoon nutmeg; two eggs; one-half cup raisins, seeded. Bake in layers and put together with white frosting.

MISS MARTHA TOWN, Black River, N. Y.

CHOCOLATE CAKE.

Two cups brown sugar; one-half cup butter; one-third cup sour milk; two eggs; two and one-half cups flour; two tablespoons grated chocolate, stirred into two-thirds cup boiling water; one teaspoon soda. This makes two layers.

FROSTING.

Two cups white sugar; one cup milk. Boil. Stir in three or four tablespoons chocolate before done.

MRS. JULIA DUNNINGTON, Redwood Falls, Minn.

MOCHA CAKE.

One and one-half cups sugar; one-half cup butter; one cup sweet milk; whites of four eggs; two cups flour; two teaspoons baking powder (level).

FILLING.

Three tablespoons coffee. Pour over this one cup boiling water; let stand until cool; strain. Add yolks of four eggs, three-fourths cup sugar, two tablespoons flour, butter size of a walnut. Boil until quite thick.

MRS. O. E. MAXON.

CHOCOLATE JUMBLES.

One cup butter; two cups sugar; four eggs; three cups flour (scant); two teaspoons baking powder; one-half teaspoon salt; two cups grated chocolate. Mix stiff enough to roll out thin. Bake about ten minutes.

MRS. D. M. CURTISS, Waseca, Minn.

JAM CAKE.

Six eggs; two cups sugar; one and one-half cups butter; six tablespoons sour cream; four cups flour; two teaspoons each allspice, cloves, cinnamon and nutmeg; two teaspoons soda; two cups jam (any kind). Add jam last. Bake in layers.

FILLING FOR CAKE.

Three cups brown sugar; one cup butter; one cup sweet cream. Cook until it hairs from spoon. Add one-half teaspoon vanilla, and beat until cool enough to spread.   MRS. L. A. WOODRUFF, Chatfield, Minn.

SPICE CAKE.

One cup sugar; one-half cup butter; one cup sour milk; one and a half cups flour; one cup raisins; one teaspoon cinnamon; one-half teaspoon cloves; one teaspoon soda; two eggs.   MRS. FRED PARSONS.

CHOCOLATE CAKE.

One cup sugar; one-half cup butter; one-half cup milk; one and three-fourths cups flour; two level teaspoons baking powder; whites of three eggs, beaten to stiff froth.

FILLING.

One square Baker's chocolate; one tablespoon butter; one-fourth cup water; one cup sugar. Boil until it threads. Pour on well-beaten yolks of three eggs; teaspoon vanilla. Beat until cold. If desired, add a few rolled nut meats. MRS. M. M. HOAGLAND.

GINGER CAKE.

One cup molasses; two-thirds cup sugar; one cup cold water; one-half cup lard or drippings; one teaspoon soda; one tablespoon ginger; flour to make not too stiff. Bake in dripping pan. MRS. J. F. REMORE.

FILLING, FROSTING, ETC.

CHOCOLATE CREAM FROSTING.

White of one egg, with an equal quantity of water. Beat egg to stiff froth. Add confectioners' sugar till thick enough to spread, flavor with vanilla, and spread on cake. Then melt one-half cake German sweet chocolate and one teaspoon boiling water. Beat well and pour over frosting. Will remain soft and creamy for a week.   MISS MARTHA TOWN.

CHOCOLATE FILLING.

One-half cup sugar; butter size of an English walnut; one and one-half bars German sweet chocolate; two-thirds cup milk. Boil until stiff enough to spread. Flavor with vanilla. Use with either loaf or layer cake.   MRS. J. B. MURRAY.

DATE FILLING.

One cup dates, seeded and chopped. Beat white of one egg very stiff. Beat into it one-half cup thick sweet cream, stir thick with powdered sugar, and add the dates. Use white icing on top, and ornament with large dates cut in halves. If you want it still better, mix chopped nut meats with dates, and also on top.
MRS. E. L. HILLYER, Minneapolis.

CREAM FROSTING.

Mix pulverized sugar with good sweet cream until you have consistency desired. Flavor with vanilla.
MISS GAFFNEY.

CREAM NUT FILLING.

Yolks of four eggs; one-half cup sugar; one cup milk; one tablespoon cornstarch; one pound English walnuts (chopped), or figs may be used. Cook until thick.

MRS. ELLA PARSONS, Klondike.

COOKED FROSTING.

One cup granulated sugar; four tablespoons water; cream tartar as large as a pea. Cook until a drop won't stick to tin dish; beat whites of two eggs to stiff froth, pour on boiling syrup, and beat until cold enough to spread on cake.

MISS MARTHA TOWN.

FILLING.

Two cups sugar; one-half cup water. Boil until it hairs. Add whites of two eggs, beaten moderately. Stir till cool. Add one-half pound chopped figs and three-quarters pound English walnuts, reserving some for top.

MRS. A. C. CHITTENDEN.

FRUIT FILLING.

Four tablespoons each of finely chopped citron and raisins; one-half cup blanched almonds, chopped; one-quarter pound finely chopped figs. Beat whites of three eggs to stiff froth; add one-half cup sugar; mix into this the chopped fruits, etc. Put between layers when cake is hot. Delicious.

ORANGE FILLING.

Juice of two oranges, with little of grated rind; one cup powdered sugar; beaten yolks of four eggs.

MRS. EDITH ARVESEN.

PEACH CREAM FILLING.

Cut or chop peaches; whip some cream; put layer of peaches, with cream, on top between each layer. Bananas, strawberries and other fruit may be used.

NUT FILLING.

One cup sugar; one cup sour cream (thick); one cup hickory nuts (chopped). Let boil few minutes. Stir a little till cool.

MRS. J. R. CONWAY.

LEMON JELLY FILLING.

One egg; one cup sugar; tablespoon butter; juice and rind of lemon. Cook till thick.

CHOCOLATE FILLING.

One cup sugar; small tablespoon flour. Mix. One-half cup milk; one-half bar sweet or eight tablespoons Baker's chocolate. Cook till thick. Add pinch soda. Take from fire and add one tablespoon cold water. Beat till cold.

MRS. W. B. THORBURN.

COOKIES AND DOUGHNUTS.

SOUR CREAM COOKIES.

Three eggs; two cups sugar; one cup sour cream; two-thirds cup butter; one teaspoon soda, and grated nutmeg. Use as little flour as you can handle to roll. Bake in quick oven.   MRS. J. L. GEE.

SUGAR COOKIES.

Two eggs; a little more than one-half cup butter; one cup sugar; one-half teaspoon soda (scant), in four tablespoons water.   MRS. NEWMAN.

MOLASSES COOKIES.

One cup butter; one cup molasses (dark); one-half teaspoon ginger; one-half teaspoon soda. Bake in sheets, after rolling quite thin. Frost with boiled frosting, then cut in squares, and if properly made will be soft and delicious.   MRS. E. L. HILLYER.

LEMON BISCUIT.

One pint new milk; one pint lard; two and one-half cups sugar; whites of two eggs; five cents' worth baker's ammonia; five cents' worth oil of lemon. Put the ammonia in a fruit can, and pour milk on it; seal up and let stand all night. In morning put together same as cookies. Do not roll as thin, but bake same as cookies. Cut with square cutter.

MISS MARTHA TOWN.

ROCKS.

One and one-half cups sugar; one cup melted butter; three large cups flour; three eggs; pinch salt; one teaspoon cinnamon; one teaspoon soda dissolved in a little warm water; one cup raisins, seeded and chopped; one pound English walnuts, chopped; two tablespoons brandy (or water). Drop from teaspoon bits size of walnut on buttered pans, and bake (not too fast). Just mix thoroughly when stirred up, but no more.
MISS MINA ROSS, St. Charles, Minn.

VANITIES.

Beat two eggs very light; add salt and flour to roll. Take piece dough large as hickory nut; roll thin as paper; fry in hot lard; sift with sugar while warm.

GRANDMA'S MOLASSES COOKIES.

One-half cup brown sugar; two cups molasses; four teaspoons soda. Put in eight tablespoons boiling water; put on one tablespoon powdered alum, eight tablespoons lard and ten tablespoons butter. Mix soft. Bake in hot oven.
MRS. GEO. H. CHAPMAN, Watertown, S. D.

GINGER COOKIES.

One cup sugar; one cup molasses; one cup shortening (butter or lard); one-half cup sour milk; one egg; one tablespoon each vinegar, ginger and soda.
MRS. BUMFORD.

7

HERMITS.

One-half cup butter; one-half cup sugar; three eggs, beaten separately; four tablespoons sour milk; one teaspoon soda; two teaspoons cinnamon; one teaspoon each cloves and allspice; one cup chopped raisins; flour until they will drop from spoon.

MRS. IDA HICKS.

GINGER COOKIES.

One cup sugar; one cup molasses; one cup butter; two eggs, well beaten; one tablespoon soda, dissolved in one-half cup hot water; one tablespoon ginger; two tablespoons cinnamon; flour to make thick enough to roll.

MRS. E. L. HEALY, Morris, Minn.

GINGER SNAPS.

Two cups molasses; one-half cup warm water; two-thirds cup melted lard; two heaping teaspoons soda; one tablespoon ginger. Mix soft.

MRS. PAGE.

DOUGHNUTS.

Two eggs; one cup sugar; one-half cup sour cream; one cup sweet milk; one-fourth teaspoon soda; one level teaspoon baking powder; pinch salt, cinnamon and nutmeg to taste. Beat well; add flour to make soft; pat out with hands.

MRS. MADISON.

DOUGHNUTS.

Break two eggs into a bowl, with one large cup sugar, one cup sour milk, one teaspoon soda. Mix very soft. They will almost turn over themselves they are so light.

MRS. STANDRING.

EGGLESS DOUGHNUTS.

One cup sour cream; two cups sour milk; one and one-half cups sugar; one teaspoon soda; salt and cinnamon to taste. Mix soft and fry in hot lard.

MRS. WATKINS.

DOUGHNUTS.

One and one-half cups sugar; one cup sweet milk; butter size of egg; two teaspoons baking powder; three eggs. Stir up and let rise one hour.

MRS. HARRIET SALISBURY.

WHITE COOKIES.

Two cups white sugar; one cup melted butter; one cup sour cream; two eggs; pinch salt; one teaspoon soda. Flour to mix soft. Roll thin and bake in quick oven.

MRS. S. GREEN.

DOUGHNUTS.

Two eggs; one cup sugar; one cup sour milk, in which has been put two tablespoons sour cream; one teaspoon soda; salt; flour to make not too stiff.

MRS. ROGERS.

GINGER SNAPS.

Two cups brown sugar; two cups butter; two cups molasses. Put the above into a pan and boil. When cold, add the rind of two lemons and one-half ounce ginger. They are very good without the lemon.

MRS. LOUISE WALTON.

OATMEAL COOKIES.

Two cups oatmeal and two cups flour. Put these together, and into the mixture rub three-fourths cup butter. Stir thoroughly into this two eggs, well beaten, with one and one-fourth cups sugar and bit of soda. Over this turn four tablespoons hot water. Flavor to taste. Bake in quick oven.

MRS. C. E. MEADER.

FRUIT COOKIES.

Yolks of two eggs; one-half cup sugar; one cup butter; one cup molasses; two teaspoons soda; one-half cup hot water; one cup raisins; one cup nuts; one teaspoon each ginger, cloves and cinnamon. Sprinkle sugar on top and frost under side. These will keep a long time.

MRS. MATTIE HUGHES, Redwood Falls, Minn.

SUGAR COOKIES.

Seven teacups flour; three cups sugar; one cup butter and lard; one cup sour milk; one teaspoon soda; three eggs; nutmeg. Roll soft.

MRS. S. N. HARRINGTON.

COOKIES.

One cup sour cream; one teaspoon soda, stirred in; one good-sized cup sugar; one egg; a little salt and nutmeg; flour to roll. MRS. R. F. WEBSTER.

PUFF-BALL DOUGHNUTS.

Three eggs; one cup sugar; one pint milk; two teaspoons baking powder; flour to permit the spoon to stand upright in mixture. Drop by dessertspoonfuls in hot lard. Will not absorb a bit of fat.

MRS. WILL GARY, Mankato, Minn.

LEMON TARTS.

Three eggs; one and one-half cups sugar; juice and rind of one lemon; one tablespoon butter; one tablespoon flour. Beat eggs and sugar together, add other ingredients, and beat again. Line patty tins with rich piecrust, fill and bake in quick oven. This will make one dozen. MRS. S. N. HARRINGTON.

NEVER-FAILING GINGER SNAPS.

One cup each sugar, molasses, and shortening; one egg; one tablespoon each ginger and vinegar, dissolving in the latter one teaspoon soda. Use no milk or water. Mix in seven cups flour and knead; roll; cut in any shape desired; bake in quick oven, taking care not to scorch. This is an excellent recipe.

MRS. WILL MULLANEY.

MY FAVORITE GINGER SNAPS.

One cup of sugar; one cup of butter; one cup of molasses; one egg; two tablespoons of vinegar. Beat butter, sugar and egg together thoroughly. Put one teaspoon of soda into molasses and beat; add this to butter and sugar; put one teaspoon of soda in the vinegar, and stir into the prepared mixture; add enough flour to roll nicely. Hard to make, but very nice.

MRS. M. A. GROESBECK, Watertown, S. D.

FRUIT COOKIES.

Two cups sugar; three eggs; one cup butter; one-half cup of New Orleans molasses; one teaspoon soda dissolved in a little water; one cup chopped raisins; one cup currants; one teaspoon cinnamon; one-half teaspoon allspice.

MRS. J. GOODWIN.

HIGH GRADE
STARCH

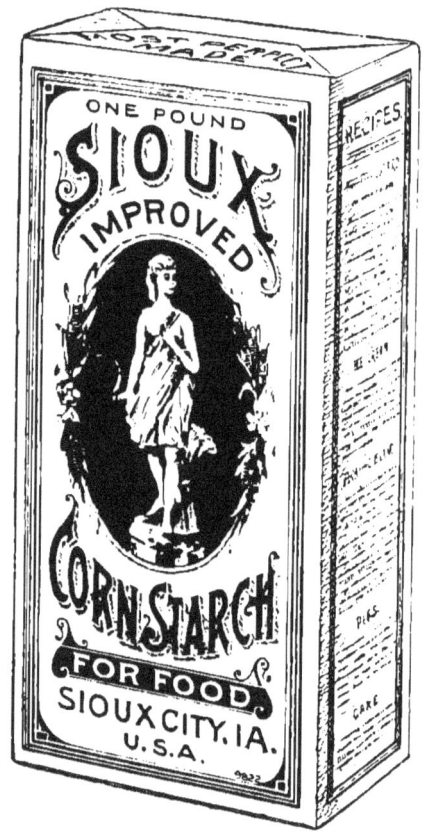

MADE BY

SIOUX CITY STARCH CO.
SIOUX CITY, IOWA.

PICKLES AND CATSUPS.

In making pickles, use oils of cloves, etc., as they don't discolor as the others do.

CUCUMBER PICKLES.

This well-tried recipe will give eminent satisfaction if exactly followed. Select small cucumbers of as even size as possible; wash them well and remove the prickles; lay 600 to 800 in jars. Scald a brine strong enough to bear up an egg, pour it over them and let them remain in it twenty-four hours, then drain and wipe each one dry. Scald as much vinegar as will cover them, and pour over them. After twenty-four hours drain this off and place the pickles in the jars or bottles in which they are to be kept. Prepare a new vinegar as follows: To each gallon of the best cider vinegar add one quart brown sugar, two large, green peppers, one teaspoon white mustard seed and an ounce each ginger root, whole cloves, allspice, stick cinnamon and black pepper; one tablespoon celery seed; alum size of a butternut; one tablespoon horseradish root, cut fine. Scald all these condiments with the vinegar and pour hot over pickles, being careful to distribute the spices through them as the receptacles are being filled. These pickles need no further care, save to keep in cool place, as the vinegar never molds, and the pickles remain as firm at close of the year as when made.

MRS. ALICE CHACE.

CHOW-CHOW.

Two quarts small, white onions; two quarts small cucumbers; two quarts string beans; two small cauliflowers; one-half dozen ripe, red peppers; one-half pound mustard seed; one pound ground mustard (which is better to get at druggist's); twenty or thirty bay leaves; two quarts good cider vinegar. Peel onions, halve cucumbers, string the beans and cut in small pieces the cauliflower. Put all in wooden bowl, and sprinkle well with salt. In morning wash and drain thoroughly, and put all into the cold vinegar, except red peppers. Let boil twenty minutes slowly, turning often. Have wax melted in dish, and as you fill bottles, cork and dip in wax. The peppers put in to show to best advantage. Is as nice as Crosse & Blackwell's "chow-chow."

MRS. ROGERS.

SPANISH PICKLE.

Two gallons sliced green tomatoes; two quarts vinegar; one quart sugar; two tablespoons each salt, ground mustard, black pepper, allspice and cloves. Mix and stew all together until tender. Stir often to prevent scorching. Can use less vinegar.

MRS. W. M. ROSS, St. Charles, Minn.

CUCUMBER PICKLE.

Take small cucumbers, wash clean and pack in fruit can. When full, put one tablespoon salt on top, and fill up with cold vinegar. Seal up. Will keep a year.

MISS MARTHA TOWN.

CUCUMBER PICKLES.

For 500 cucumbers about a finger long: Three quarts salt; three gallons vinegar; five ounces alum; one-half pound sugar; one ounce allspice; three-quarters ounce cloves; one-quarter pound pepper and horseradish. Dissolve salt in boiling water enough to cover cucumbers. Let stand over night. In morning drain and wipe. Put spices, etc., into vinegar. Let boil, and put onto cucumbers. Put horseradish in in pieces (not too much). Will keep for two or three years. An old and well tried recipe.

MRS. F. P. WILLARD, Russell, Minn.

MIXED PICKLE.

One colander of sliced green tomatoes; one colander of cucumbers pared and sliced; one quart sliced onions; two good handfuls salt. Let all stand over night. In morning drain through sieve. Take one gallon vinegar, one pound brown sugar, one teacup white mustard seed, one-half cup celery seed, one tablespoon black pepper, two tablespoons ground mustard, one teaspoon allspice. Let come just to boil, and pour over tomatoes, etc., hot. Tried, and never found wanting.

MRS. WILL ROGERS.

PICKLED ONIONS.

Use small onions, pour boiling water over and peel. Leave in salt water over night. Next morning steam until they can be pierced with fork. Put in jar, and turn hot spiced vinegar over.

MRS. SARAH A. WATSON, River Falls, Wis.

SWEET TOMATO PICKLE.

One peck green tomatoes; six large onions; one cup salt. Stand over night; drain. Cover with two quarts water, one quart vinegar. Let boil fifteen minutes; drain. Then take two quarts vinegar, one tablespoon cloves, two tablespoons each allspice, ginger, mustard and cinnamon, and one teaspoon cayenne pepper. Put in pickles, and boil fifteen minutes.

MRS. JOS. ADDISON.

CHOPPED TOMATO PICKLE.

One peck green tomatoes, chopped fine as desired. Mix with one cup salt, and let stand over night. Drain well. Two quarts vinegar; three cups sugar; three-quarters cup white mustard seed; two dessert spoons each ground cloves and cinnamon; one dessert spoon allspice. Boil chopped tomatoes in this one-half hour; put in jars and keep cool.

MRS. F. M. HEALY.

COMBINATION PICKLE.

Three quarts ripe tomatoes, peeled and chopped; one-half pint grated horseradish; one pint celery, chopped; one-half cup chopped onions; eight table-spoons each mustard seed, sugar and salt; two table-spoons chopped green peppers; one tablespoon ground cinnamon; one teaspoon each cloves and mace; one quart vinegar. Mix all together. Needs no cooking. Will keep in any jar without sealing.

MISS MARTHA TOWN, Black River, N. Y.

CUCUMBER PICKLES.

Cover with boiling water; let them stand until cool, or next morning; drain. To every gallon of vinegar put two tablespoons white mustard seed, one of alum, two-thirds cup salt, a good handful horseradish roots. Pour over cucumbers in jar. Good in few days, or will keep a year.   MRS. LARABEE.

SALT CUCUMBER PICKLES.

Soak salted cucumbers over night in fresh water. In morning take out of water, and steam fifteen minutes; put in jar. Put one cup sugar and a small handful of mixed spices. Pour over cold vinegar.
                          MRS. S. G. MARSHALL.

SWEET PICKLE.

To seven pounds fruit use one pound sugar and one tablespoon each of cloves, cinnamon, allspice, pepper and salt, and just vinegar enough to cover fruit when wilted by boiling. Boil all together till tender.
                          MRS. C. H. RICHARDSON.

GREEN TOMATO SWEET PICKLE.

To seven pounds tomatoes, three pounds sugar and one pint vinegar, add one tablespoon each of all kinds spices. Steam the tomatoes until tender. Scald vinegar, sugar and spices together, and pour over tomatoes. Do this three mornings in succession.
                          MRS. C. H. RICHARDSON.

MUSTARD PICKLE.

Four cauliflowers, cut up; one-half peck white onions; one-half peck cucumbers; six green peppers; a few green tomatoes. Let stand in salt over night. Drain next morning. Add one gallon best vinegar. Let them come to scald; then add a paste made of one-half cup flour, three cups sugar, one ounce tumeric, one-half ounce mustard. Cook a few minutes and bottle.

MRS. E. J. WAKEMAN.

CHOW-CHOW.

One peck green tomatoes; three heads cabbage; six red peppers; three heads cauliflower. Chop fine and sprinkle with pint of salt. Let stand twenty-four hours. Drain thoroughly. Place in kettle with two pounds brown sugar, one ounce each of white mustard seed, black pepper and celery seed. Cover with strong vinegar and boil till clear. Onion may be added if desired.

MRS. D. G. STEWART, Canton, Minn.

KANSAS PICKLE.

One hundred cucumbers, three inches long; slice with skins on; twenty-five small onions, sliced. Layer cucumbers, then onions; sprinkle with salt. Let stand three hours; drain well. Then take one cup salad oil, two cups each white and black mustard seed, four tablespoons celery seed, four quarts cold vinegar. Stir well, pour over pickles and cover tight.

MRS. O. PEHRSON.

CHILE SAUCE.

Take two quarts ripe tomatoes, four large onions and four red peppers. Chop them together; then add four cups vinegar, three tablespoons each cloves, ground cinnamon, ginger, allspice and nutmeg. Boil all together for one hour, and bottle after straining through sieve or coarse netting. Is equal to famous Worcestershire.

OLD ENGLISH CHILE SAUCE.

Remove the skins from twenty-four ripe tomatoes. Chop together with one onion, two peppers. Add two tablespoons each salt and sugar, one tablespoon each cloves, allspice and cinnamon and one quart vinegar. Boil two hours. Put in jars.

MRS. JOS. ADDISON.

CATSUP.

One peck of tomatoes. Boil till soft, then run through sieve. Add one teacup sugar, one quart vinegar, two tablespoons ground mustard, two tablespoons white pepper, one teaspoon cayenne pepper, one teaspoon cloves, two teaspoons cinnamon and four tablespoons salt. Let boil away half.

MRS. W. B. THORBURN.

JELLIES AND PRESERVES.

STEWED CRANBERRIES.

One pound cranberries, washed and picked over carefully; one pound granulated sugar; one-half pint water. Place water and sugar on stove to boil. When boiling put in berries. They will soon heat through and begin to burst. Stir continually until well cooked, which will take about ten minutes after all begins to boil. Dip mold in cold water and turn berries in; set till following day. The above makes them neither too sweet nor too sour. Will turn out like jelly; is nicer to eat with game or poultry, as you have full berry. One can prepare several pounds at a time, as it keeps perfectly, by pasting paper over dishes, for six or eight weeks.

SELECTED.

LEMON JELLY.

Dissolve one-half box gelatine in one cup cold water; grate yellow rind of two lemons, take off thick skin, and grate the pulp; put three cups water in granite kettle; add three even cups sugar; let boil few minutes; add pulp and rind and gelatine; put into mold and set in cool place.

BAKED PIEPLANT.

Cut in pieces about an inch long; put in baking dish in layers with an equal weight of sugar; cover closely and bake.

MRS. THORBURN.

PIEPLANT PRESERVES.

Wash clean, but do not peel; cut an inch or two in length; put a layer in small jar, then layer of sugar; another layer of pieplant, then sugar, until jar is full, allowing pound of sugar to pound of pieplant. Cover tightly, put in hot oven, and as soon as it is heated through it is done. Do not put in a drop of water. An earthen bean pot is best to use, with cover. Fruit must then cook one-half hour. Put up in glass cans.

PIEPLANT JELLY.

Gather, wash and cut pieplant in small pieces (do not remove skin); put into kettle with very little water, and cook until very tender; pour into a jelly bag and let it drain; return to kettle before it cools. Boil one-half hour as hard as it can boil, then measure, and add as much sugar as there is juice after it has boiled.

MRS. W. PIERSON.

GRAPE-CITRON PRESERVES.

Prepare citrons (thoroughly ripe) by paring and cutting into small cubes. Steam over hot water until tender; drain and weigh, then drop into hot syrup, allowing pound of granulated sugar to pound of fruit, and place over slow fire. Fill a basin with Concord grapes, and place over fire, letting them cook in their own juice until seeds and skins are cooked free from pulp, then put through fine sieve or fruit squeezer. Of this grape marmalade just prepared add to the citron a sufficient amount to color a bright red or purple, as the grapes may differ in color. Cook slowly until citron is clear, and of a bright, even color, and this will give a flavor both delicate and palatable.

MRS. C. E. MEADER, Canton, Minn.

8

ICE CREAM AND OTHER ICES.

TUTTI FRUTTI ICE CREAM.

Two quarts rich cream; one pound pulverized sugar; four whole eggs. Mix well together, place on fire, stir constantly and bring to a boiling point. Remove, and stir until cold. Flavor with one teaspoon of vanilla. Place in freezer, and when half frozen add one pound preserved fruits, peaches, apricots, cherries, pineapple, etc. All of these fruits are to be cut up in small pieces.   MRS. CYRUS P. SHEPARD.

PINEAPPLE SPONGE.

One can grated pineapple; one cup sugar; one and a half cups water; one-half box gelatine; whites of four eggs. Soak gelatine in one cup water. Put other one-half cup water on sugar; put on stove; dissolve, adding gelatine and pineapple; strain through cloth, and set away to cool. When a little stiff, add beaten whites of eggs. Beat all together thoroughly, turn in mold, and set in cold place. Serve with cream.

MRS. S. N. HARRINGTON.

SHERBET.

Three cups sugar. Add one quart boiling water and boil for a few moments. When cool, add the juice of four lemons and a little more water. This may be varied by adding the juice of an orange, or mashed peaches during the peach season. It is particularly nice with the addition of some pitted cherries and one tablespoon almond flavoring.

MRS. E. W. MAHONEY.

CURRANT COZMIA.

Five pounds currants; five pounds sugar; one pound seeded raisins; one pound English walnuts, chopped fine; grated rind and juice of one lemon; juice of four oranges and rind of three oranges. Boil rind in three or four different waters, to extract the oil. Boil until as thick as preserves, and when nearly done, add a dash of brandy.

MRS. C. A. COOK, Bloomington, Ill.

LEMON SHERBET.

Juice of four lemons; two cups granulated sugar; one quart of fresh milk and one teaspoon lemon extract.

MRS. F. S. WETHERBEE.

TUTTI FRUTTI ICE CREAM (UNCOOKED).

One quart cream; whites of three eggs, beaten very light; four tablespoonfuls sugar; one-half teaspoonful vanilla. Whip cream before freezing, and add ten cents' worth candied cherries, one teacup grated pineapple and one teacup English walnuts and almonds, mixed.

MRS. CYRUS P. SHEPPARD.

SPANISH CREAM.

One-half box gelatine; soak in little cold water. One quart milk; let come to boiling point; four eggs, beaten separately. Add one cup sugar to yolks, and two tablespoons warm milk. Add gelatine to milk; then sugar and yolks. Let cook little. Remove from fire and add whites of eggs. Flavor with vanilla, lemon or almond. Cool in molds.

MRS. E. J. WAKEMAN.

GRAPE SHERBET.

Sweeten one quart grape juice to taste. Add one cup sugar to two cups orange juice and stir until sugar is dissolved. Add to the grape juice. Turn into the freezer and freeze. When nearly frozen, remove dasher and beat in with a spoon the white of one egg, beaten light, with two tablespoons powdered sugar. Beat well. MRS. R. R. BUMFORD.

ORANGE SHERBET.

Juice of four lemons; grated rind and juice of one orange; two cups of sugar, and one quart of rich milk. Have freezer packed and all ingredients very cold. Mix ingredients together in freezer and freeze quickly. MRS. WM. EVERETT, Waseca. Minn.

MILK SHERBET.

Boil one quart rich milk with the rind of one lemon and one pound sugar. When cold, put in freezer and half freeze. Then add whites of three eggs and juice of four lemons, with a little more sugar mixed with the lemon juice. MRS. R. R. BUMFORD.

CRANBERRY ICE.

Two quarts of cranberries. Sweeten with sugar, boil and strain. Add juice and pulp of two oranges, juice of two lemons, then freeze. If too strong of cranberry, add water. MRS. CYRUS P. SHEPARD.

CHOCOLATE ICE CREAM.

For one gallon: Five yolks of eggs, well beaten; three pints new milk; two coffee cups sugar; two squares grated chocolate (Baker's). Cook smooth in double boiler. When ready to freeze, add three pints cream, well beaten, and whites of five eggs, beaten stiff. Flavor with vanilla. MRS. JOHN L. WATSON.

PEACH ICE CREAM.

Scald one quart cream (or one-half pint milk may be used instead of one-half pint of cream). Add one cup of sugar. Peel and slice a full quart of fine ripe peaches. Sweeten well, and add when cream is partly frozen. Allow an hour for cream to ripen after freezing. MRS. EDITH ARVESEN.

COFFEE CREAM.

One and a half cups cream; one cup strong, hot coffee; one-half cup water; one-half cup sugar; three-quarters ounce gelatine. Soak gelatine in water till dissolved; pour into the coffee; add sugar; cool and strain, and stir in cream, which should be whipped before adding. Fill molds, and set in cold place over night. MRS. F. C. WHITNEY.

PINEAPPLE ICE.

Three and a half pints sugar; three and a half quarts water; one can grated pineapple. When nearly frozen, fill with whipped cream and freeze. MRS. O. E. MAXSON.

Testimonial.

We have used this Cocoa and have found it all that it is recommended to be.

Mrs. J. W. Williams.
Mrs. F. M. Healy.

BEVERAGES.

RASPBERRY SHRUB.

Place red raspberries in a stone jar, cover them with good cider vinegar, and let stand over night. Next morning strain, and to one pint of juice add one pint sugar. Boil ten minutes, and bottle while hot.

MRS. W. C. KAYSER.

SODA WATER.

One-quarter pound tartaric acid; whites of five eggs; five pounds white sugar; two quarts water; one ounce wintergreen essence. Let come to a boil; then bottle. To prepare the drink use two tablespoons syrup to glass of cold water; stir in one-quarter teaspoon soda. Put wintergreen in after it has boiled.

MRS. THORBURN.

MAKE TEA.

Have teapot hot. Use small teaspoon tea for each person. Pour on boiling water, and let stand on back ov stove from seven to ten minutes. Do not boil.

HOME-MADE WINE.

GRAPE, CURRANT, ELDERBERRY, ETC.

One quart clear juice; two quarts soft water; three pounds sugar. Put into large jar. Keep in warm place. As it works, skim. When through working, bottle. Put a part of water on pulp, and strain again.

MRS. ROGERS.

TO MAKE COFFEE.

First, use good coffee; second, have it ground fine. Use one heaping teaspoon for each person. Put on about one cup of cold water for three or four teaspoons; put on stove; let come to boil. Pour on boiling water to make desired amount. Let stand on back of stove few minutes.

PUNCH.

Six glasses jelly, three of currant and three of crab-apple. Whip to a froth, adding gradually one pint boiling water to each glass jelly. Add juice of one and a half dozen lemons, six cups sugar and juice of six oranges. Add cold water to make three gallons. Serve ice cold.

CANDIES.

CREAM CANDY.

First, get your flavorings, colorings and manilla paper ready. Have also a little melted chocolate, nuts and dates. The English walnut is the best to use; the broken pieces can be chopped with figs, and is nice for filling some. Take a new basin, two cups granulated sugar, one-half cup of water and a very little pinch of cream of tartar. Then put it on to boil. Do not stir after it commences to boil. Let it boil until it threads from a spoon. You must be careful not to let it burn. When you think it has boiled long enough, so that when stirred it will grain, set it away to cool. You commence to stir until it grains. It is now ready for the hands. Divide into as many bunches as you want colors, but save the most of white. Flavor and color each bunch to suit the taste. Be careful not to color too highly. Mix each bunch well. It cannot be mixed too much. The chocolate can now be used in coloring.

The shaping is the next thing.

For strawberries, color red and shape like the berry, then roll in red sand sugar.

For the striped, mold a little bunch of three or four colors in flat stripes, and lay one upon the other, then roll up and slice off with a thin, sharp knife.

Form some in round flat bunches, and put half a walnut on the top. Fill dates with some, and press nearly together. If the candy has boiled just right, you can make in desired shape. You have put too much water with it if it does not grain.

MRS. A. J. CHAMBERLAIN.

MARSHMALLOWS.

Take two ounces fine white, powdered gum arabic. Cover it with eight tablespoons of water. Let it stand for one hour, then set the vessel in boiling water and stir until the gum is dissolved. Strain through cheese-cloth into a double boiler, and add seven ounces of powdered sugar. Stir this over the fire until the mixture is white and stiff. This takes at least forty-five minutes. Then stir in hastily the well beaten whites of four eggs. Take it from the fire, beat rapidly for about two minutes, and add a teaspoonful of vanilla extract. Dust a square tin pan with cornstarch, pour in the mixture, and stand in a cool place. When cold, cut in squares.

FRANCES BLANCHE HILLYER, Minneapolis.

FUDGES.

Three cups light brown sugar; one-half cup hot water; butter size of an egg; two tablespoons grated Baker's chocolate. Boil until, when dripping from spoon, the mixture threads. Add one teaspoon vanilla extract and two teaspoons of cream. Stir until cool.

FRANCES BLANCHE HILLYER, Minneapolis.

CARAMELS.

One cup brown sugar; one cup sweet cream; one cup white sugar; one cup molasses; six ounces of chocolate; butter size of hickory nut. Boil until done, pour into buttered tins and cut.

MRS. FREMONT HOAGLAND.

CREAM DATES.

Put the whites of two eggs in a dish with equal quantities of cold water. Add a teaspoon of vanilla extract, and beat until it froths. Add sufficient powdered sugar to make a stiff paste, work the mixture until smooth, form into tiny, oblong rolls and press them into the center of the dates, from which the stones were removed. Press the halves together, roll in sugar, and set away to harden.

MRS. W. F. BRYANT.

PRALINES.

One cup brown sugar; one-quarter cup milk; one teaspoon butter; one cup English walnut meats. Cook until it hairs, or threads, then stir in the nut meats, either whole or chopped.

MRS. HATTIE WOODRUFF WILLIAMS, Chatfield, Minn.

MAPLE NUT TAFFY.

Two pounds maple sugar; one pint water. Boil, without stirring, till brittle when dropped in cold water. When done, add one tablespoon vinegar. Have ready buttered tins, lined with nuts, and pour candy over them. When partly cool mark off into strips or stamp with dies.

FUDGES.

One cup milk; two cups sugar; one-quarter cake Baker's chocolate; butter size of a walnut. Boil about twenty minutes, stir slowly all the time, pour in buttered pans one-half inch thick, let cool, and cut in diamonds or squares.

MRS. T. A. WOODRUFF, Chatfield, Minn.

MENU FOR FIRST PRIZE DINNER.

Puree of Split Peas.   Croutons.

Fried or Sautéd Fish.   Sauce Tartare.

Potato Roses.

Boned Fowl, Steamed.   Rice Stuffing.

Cream Sauce.   Buttered Onions.

Lettuce Salad.

Crackers.   Cheese.

Sponge Cream Boxes.

Coffee.

Puree of Split Peas.—Crack the bones of the chicken, cover with water, and simmer gently four hours. At the first boil, skim, and at the end of the third hour, add one teaspoon salt, one-quarter of an onion with two cloves stuck in it, one-half teaspoon celery seed, or a sprig of dried celery top, one-quarter of a sliced carrot and turnip, one-half bay leaf, one-quarter teaspoon whole pepper. At the end of fourth hour strain stock. When cold, remove the fat from surface. Cover one cup split peas with cold water and soak over night. In morning wash through several waters, then cover with pint of water and simmer two hours. Press through colander, then add one cup of stock and press through puree sieve. Add another cup stock, and return to fire. Rub together one-half teaspoon flour and one tablespoon butter. Stir into puree and stir until perfectly smooth. Now add one-half teaspoon salt, one-quarter teaspoon pepper, one teaspoon grated onion. Boil gently five minutes, stirring all the time. Serve in tureen with croutons.

Sauce Tartare.—Make one-half cup mayonnaise with tarragon vinegar and a little onion juice. Just before serving add one-half teaspoon each parsley and capers, chopped fine.

Sautéd Fish.—Wash and dry the fish, sprinkle with salt and pepper and roll in flour. Put salt pork grease in a frying pan, and when it is hot lay in fish and cook until it is amber color on each side.

Potato Roses.—To one cup of seasoned, mashed potatoes add one beaten egg and beat well together. Put the mixture in a pastry bag with a star-shaped opening, and press it through. As it comes through the tube guide it in a circle till it comes to a point. Save a little of the egg, and brush each rose with it. Place a bit of butter on each one, and brown in oven.

Cream Sauce.—Make a roux of one tablespoon of butter and one of flour. Add a cup of milk, salt and pepper to taste, and the finely chopped gizzard and heart of the fowl. Let it boil up and serve.

Boned Fowl.—Bone a two-pound fowl. Wash and wipe dry. Dust the inside with half a teaspoon of salts, one-quarter teaspoon pepper, and stuff with a cup of boiled rice, with tablespoon butter mixed with it. Dust outside with salt and pepper; tie in cheesecloth. Steam until tender.

Buttered Onions.—Boil four good-sized onions or eight smaller ones in salted water until tender. Drain, and dress with a salt spoon of white pepper, one of salt, and two tablespoons of melted butter.

Lettuce Salad.—Wash the lettuce carefully and put in ice water until serving time. Then toss it in a clean towel until dry. Serve with a French dressing.

Sponge Cream Boxes.—Make a sponge cake as follows: Beat the yolk of an egg until thick, then add gradually one-half cup of finely granulated sugar. Then add alternately, in small quantities, two tablespoons of water and one-half cup flour which has been sifted with one-half teaspoon of baking powder, flavor with one-half teaspoon lemon extract, and lastly fold in the beaten white of an egg. Bake in a shallow tin, six inches square. Bake the day before using. Cut the cake into four square pieces, split each piece, and cut the top parts into four strips each. Stick these strips with a little sugar, cooked to a soft ball, to the sides of the square bottom pieces, thus forming shallow boxes. Fill these boxes with half a pint of whipped cream, sweetened with two tablespoons of sugar and flavored with one-half teaspoon of vanilla.

From November Ladies' Home Journal.

LUNCHEON FOR FORTY PERSONS.

FIRST COURSE.

Escalloped Salmon or Crab.   Tiny Tim Pickles.

Sliced Bread and Butter.

SECOND COURSE.

Sliced Ham and Tongue, garnished with Parsley.

Saratoga Chips.   Pineapple Jelly.

Rolls and Coffee.

THIRD COURSE.

Chicken Salad.   Salted Wafers and Olives.

FOURTH COURSE.

Angel's Food.   Layer Cake.

Ice Cream and Strawberries.

Quantity of material for above:
Two quarts sweet cream.
Escalloped Fish.—Four cans fish; one quart bread crumbs; one pint cream.
Two bottles Tiny Tims.
Two small loaves of bread, cut thin and buttered.
Seven pounds boiled ham.
Two small beef tongues.

Two boxes Saratoga chips.

Sixty rolls.

Pineapple Jelly.—Two boxes gelatine; one can pineapple; three lemons.

One pound best coffee.

Three chickens; three large heads celery; dressing made of two dozen yolks of eggs and one cup cream.

One pound salted wafers.

Two bottles olives (forty in each).

Three pounds fine butter.

Three dozen eggs.

Two angel's foods.

Two small layer cakes.

Two gallons ice cream.

Seven quarts fresh strawberries.

If ice cream is prepared at home, more cream and milk will be needed; also, ice and common salt.

MRS. JAMES BURCHARD.

9

MISCELLANEOUS.

CLEANSING FLUID.

Four ounces ammonia; four ounces white castile soap; two ounces each alcohol, glycerine and ether. Cut soap fine; dissolve in one quart water over fire; add four quarts water. When nearly cold add other ingredients. This will make nearly eight quarts, and will cost about seventy-five cents. Put in bottle and stopper tight. It will keep good any length of time. Nice to wash all woolen goods; invaluable for removing marks on furniture. To wash goods, use about one cup of fluid to a pail of luke-warm water, rinse well in plenty of clear water, and iron on wrong side while damp. For coat collars, etc., take little fluid in cup; apply with clean rag; wipe well with second clean rag. It will make woolens look bright.

DIRECTIONS FOR WASHING FABRICS CONTAINING WOOL.

Soak thirty minutes in warm soap suds. Next wash in clean soap suds by squeezing with your hands—no rubbing. Rinse well in warm water, lay out the garment on a board or table, and give it its original shape by forming by hand; then hang up lengthwise to dry, and iron while slightly damp. Keep the temperature of the different waters about the same. Don't wash in water used for other clothes. Don't rub soap on the garment. Avoid patent wash powders and all soap containing alkali. A good olive oil soap is the best.

YEAST.

One gallon water; five cents' worth hops. Let boil good; strain, and add five potatoes grated and one large tablespoon flour; stir, and let just boil up; turn into crock. Add one cup sugar (white), and, when cool enough, one yeast cake which has been dissolved in little warm water. Let rise; stir down once; put in jug with one-half cup salt. Don't put cork in tight for several hours, or you will have an explosion. Will keep several weeks in cool place.   MRS. ROGERS.

TO CLEAN CARPETS AND RUGS.

Two bars of Ivory soap (shaved) in one gallon of soft water; four ounces borax; sixteen ounces salsoda; four ounces pulverized fuller's earth. Boil to mix. Remove from fire, and add nine gallons of cold water. Apply freely to rug, and scrub with soft brush. Wipe off foam with dry cloth.   MRS. A. BLANCHARD.

TO RENEW BLACK LACE.

Sponge thoroughly on both sides with alcohol; then wrap and pin round a bottle, and leave until thoroughly dry.   MRS. HOLCOMB, Bloomington, Ill.

REMOVE MILDEW.

Wet in rain water; rub the spots with soap and chalk; lay in dew and sun two or three days and nights; rub thoroughly with soap and chalk once or twice a day.

WASHING FLUID.

Soda borax, one ounce; ammonia carbonate, two ounces; washing soda, one and a half pounds; Babbitt's potash, one can. Mix in one gallon of cold, soft water, stir until dissolved, then bottle. Use two-thirds cup to two pails of water. Soak clothes over night; then wring out; soap well, and put into boiler which has this fluid in water, and boil ten minutes; take out, suds well and rinse.   NELLIE M. BAKER.

RECIPE FOR RENOVENE.

Six bars Ivory soap; six gallons soft water; one pound borax; five cents' worth glycerine; ten cents' worth ammonia; ten cents' worth oil sassafras. Dissolve the soap in water, and add borax while hot. When cold add other stuff, and let it get cold.

PICKLE FOR HAMS OR BEEF.

For 100 pounds meat, seven pounds coarse salt, two pounds brown sugar, one quart molasses, one-quarter pound saltpeter, one-half pound soda, six gallons soft water. Let come to boil, and skim. Let cool. Put in meat for thirty days.   MRS. THORBURN.

BAKING POWDER.

Six ounces tartaric acid, eight ounces best baking soda, and one quart best patent flour. Sift five or six times through fine sieve so as to thoroughly mix. Keep well corked, and use same quantity as other powder.

TO REMOVE STAINS.

Cocoa stains can be removed from linen by washing with Ivory soap and cold water.

Ink stains can be removed by dipping the spotted part in tallow, melted. Wash out the tallow, and the ink will disappear.

REMOVE IRON RUST.

Juice of lemon and salt placed on spot, and fabric placed in sun, will remove rust.

TO KILL PLANT LICE.

Cigar ashes will kill lice on rose bushes without injuring plant. I have tried it in many instances with great success.

To clean lace curtains without washing, shake gently to remove loose dust; then spread a clean sheet on floor, and lay the curtains one above the other, with a plentiful sprinkling of bran between them. Roll them up tightly; put away in dry place for week or ten days; then shake the bran out, and with a moderately hot iron press out wrinkles, and your curtains are as nice as new.

To remove kerosene oil from carpets, cover stain with bran, and let remain twenty-four hours, or until oil is absorbed.

Care should be taken of gasoline, as it is a deadly poison.